CVC
4

CVC

Carter V. Cooper

SHORT FICTION ANTHOLOGY SERIES

BOOK FOUR

SELECTED BY AND WITH A PREFACE BY

Gloria Vanderbilt

EXILE
editions

Library and Archives Canada Cataloguing in Publication

CVC / Gloria Vanderbilt, editor.

(Carter V. Cooper short fiction anthology series ; book four) Issued in print and electronic formats.
ISBN 978-1-55096-421-9 (pbk.).--ISBN 978-1-55096-424-0 (pdf).--
ISBN 978-1-55096-422-6 (epub).--ISBN 978-1-55096-423-3 (mobi)

1. Short stories, Canadian (English). 2. Canadian fiction (English)--21st century. I. Vanderbilt, Gloria, 1924-, editor II. Title. III. Series: Carter V. Cooper short fiction anthology series ; bk. 4

PS8329.1.C834 2014   C813'.010806   C2014-903245-5
                                                 C2014-903246-3

Copyright © with the Authors, and Exile Editions, 2014
Design and Composition by Hourglass Angels mc
Typeset in Garamond, Mona Lisa and Trajan fonts
Printed by Imprimerie Gauvin

Published by Exile Editions Ltd ~ www.ExileEditions.com
144483 Southgate Road 14 – GD, Holstein, Ontario, N0G 2A0
Printed and Bound in Canada in 2014

The publisher would like to acknowledge the financial support of the Canada Council for the Arts, the Government of Canada through the Canada Book Fund (CBF), the Ontario Arts Council, and the Ontario Media Development Corporation, for our publishing activities.

  Conseil des Arts du Canada   Canada Council for the Arts

ONTARIO ARTS COUNCIL
CONSEIL DES ARTS DE L'ONTARIO

 Canada

Ontario
Ontario Media Development Corporation

Canadian Sales: The Canadian Manda Group, 165 Dufferin Street, Toronto ON M6K 3H6   www.mandagroup.com   416 516 0911

North American and international Distribution, and U.S. Sales:
Independent Publishers Group, 814 North Franklin Street,
Chicago IL 60610   www.ipgbook.com   toll free: 1 800 888 4741

In memory of

Carter V. Cooper

The Winners for Year Four

Best Story by an Emerging Writer
≈ $10,000 ≈
Jason Timermanis

Best Story by a Writer at Any Point of Career
≈ $5,000 ≈
Hugh Graham

CVC
BOOK FOUR

Preface by Gloria Vanderbilt
11

Jason Timermanis
15

Hugh Graham
24

Helen Marshall
43

K'ari Fisher
74

Linda Rogers
90

Susan P. Redmayne
100

Matthew R. Loney
118

Erin Soros
141

Gregory Betts
162

George M{c}Whirter
178

Madeline Sonik
188

Leon Rooke
196

Authors' Biographies
215

PREFACE

I am proud and thrilled that all these wonderful writers are presented in this edition of the *CVC Anthology*. Though I, and those who loved Carter, still hear his voice in our heads and in our hearts, my son's voice was silenced long ago. I hope this prize helps other writers find their voice, and helps them touch others' lives with the mystery and magic of the written word. And so, as we conclude our fourth year of this annual short fiction competition – open to all Canadian writers – I have awarded two prizes: $10,000 for the best story by an emerging writer, and $5,000 for the best story by a writer at any point of her/his career. Hundreds of stories were received in 2013-14, and from the 12 that eventually were shortlisted, I selected the winners, being those that most appealed to me, as a writer, as a reader, and as a lover of the written word on paper. About the winners, I have this to say: "Appetite" by the new writer Jason Timermanis is a story that rings into the gut with the strength of Shirley Jackson's "The Lottery." The writing is taut, compelling, mounting in terror. Masterful. And it stays with me, deeply; I cannot stop myself from thinking about it. Hugh Graham's "The Man" is a gripping, moving vision of childhood remembered, free from the fake lyricism that often infects such stories. Wise without being clever. The paranoia is never milked. A work, as Ford Madox Ford liked to say, that is of the "First Chop."

And I want to give a big *Thank You* to the readers who adjudicated this competition: Matt Shaw, Joe Fiorito, Norman Snider and Barry Callaghan... all who have played their own special roles in the development and support of emerging writers.

Gloria Vanderbilt
May, 2014

Jason Timermanis

APPETITE

The man awakens to murmuring outside his door, and is certain it's the village men, come to slit his throat and leave him bleeding beneath the saguaros. He lifts his head from the pillow to listen, trying to tease out a strand of conversation, and hears the voice of one, then several women. His lungs ease open at the sound, release like two clenched fists. They would never kill him in the presence of women.

He rises to open the door and the morning sun pours in from off the desert hills. All the people of the village are there, standing in loose clusters; they gape at him and point their fingers. He looks out and sees the woman at the back of the crowd, behind her father. The men of her family could have killed him quietly on one of the trails, but instead they stand and watch. Fingers keep pointing until the man turns and sees what has brought them all.

There are marks on the front of his door. Seven of them, spread along the wood in smears of pulpy white. It takes him a moment to believe they're really there, that the old stories have come to life on his door. He leans forward and breathes in. They do smell of milk.

Men appear from the side of his house, leading his only horse away, and satisfied that he's seen the marks, the crowd turns and follows them back down the hill. They leave the man to frown in the sun, breathing in the smell of milk, as the woman looks over her shoulder and burns him with her gaze.

The next morning, he is still sleeping when some of the villagers return to take his door off its hinges and cut out the dirty glass from the single window on the side of his house. Standing at the end of his cot are men he once knew well, before he came and went so many times that no one thought of him as local anymore. He'd hoped this most recent return had gone unnoticed.

As soon as he rises, they carry his cot out of the house. The chest of drawers is next; a relic from his grandfather; the old wood splits as they lift it. Women are tossing the contents of the kitchen cupboards into sacks. They look at him then look away. The men stare and wait. He knows what they're waiting for, and slowly he obliges. He slides out of his shirt, revealing a torso bony from months on the road, eating little more than jerky. He removes his shorts; a pair of underwear comes off last, balled up and handed to them. They take his boots from the front door then leave with their women. Naked, he watches them drag their sacks down the hill.

Of everything they take, it's only the door they're careful with. Each corner rests on a man's shoulder, the marks facing upwards to the sun. They will bury it tenderly, as though it were a child, under the largest olive tree in the graveyard, where the other doors have been buried for as long as anyone can remember. Where the smell of milk never stays below the ground.

Down the hill from the man's house is another house, with no doors and no windows. When the village boys stand at the edge of the trail, and the afternoon light is falling, they can see into the house and its sand-filled rooms.

The man only dimly remembers the family that lived there decades ago – the wife and young daughter who were driven from the village the day the house was emptied, and the husband who was left behind, naked in the doorway. They say he had been an industrious man, spending his days collecting the monsoon rains in barrels to keep alive a cluster of date palms he'd planted at the edge of the village on a streak of untouched land. When he was gone, the little date palms curled in on themselves and blackened.

Along the house's overhang, six rusted forks twist on frayed bits of rope. Many more forks have fallen, to lie under the dunes around the house, and around the other empty houses that dot the village. When the winds shift, a few of them surface, furred red with rust, like bloodied teeth peeking out from the sand.

The man turns his gaze from the empty house to find sunlight pooling on his dirt floor. With the filthy glass removed from the window, the light falls brightly for the first time. It feels like a visitor. From a distance, children watch him through the window, quietly whispering between themselves about his naked body lit white as he leans into the sun.

In the night, the sand comes through the doorway, spinning in loose circles around the man's sleeping body. It silently gathers in the corners of his room.

Each day a different group of women come, their men waiting outside, to spit and argue under the shade of the ragged palms. The whole village smells of cooking meat.

"Rump roast stew," the first woman says, placing a small cauldron in the centre of the room. He doesn't recognize the other women, but he remembers her: a friend of his grandmother's, once. She's built more solidly than most women in the village, and shifts from one sturdy foot to the other, glancing every now and then out the window, as they all do, up into the hills. Their eyes look for approval. This woman is amused by his nakedness. She leans forward to follow the curve of his spine as he hunches over the cauldron to eat. He can feel the weight of her eyes on his crotch.

There is enough food in the cauldron for three men. It takes him the morning to eat it all, and the women wait, sitting on their heels, unmoving as statues. Sauce drips into the hair of his thighs. He chews and thinks of his horse, its greasy neck and the dull sheen of its eyes when spying an apple. His horse lies dismembered in kitchens across the village now, and its flanks fill his belly. The villagers provide him no water to wash away the taste.

Ribs follow the next day, brought by an old schoolteacher with wrinkles hardened into cracks across her face. She says, "I char ribs black on both sides then rub in chilies – chilies from my garden, not from market."

He thanks the women after each meal. As they carry out the bones, they leave footprints in the thin carpet of sand on the floor.

In the days that pass, he is fed the flank, the T-bone, the skirt and, one grimly memorable afternoon, the rubbery intestines, piled high on a platter, "stuffed with dates, soaked in lemon and fried with almonds." They bunched in his throat and he retched; still, he continued, as black smoke rose from behind the hills. They were burning his possessions and singing. Their high, crooked voices raised a song of offering into the hills. What they offered was him.

One night, he dreams of the woman's father, with his grim, straight mouth, standing outside the house, twisting a coil of rope in his hands. He knows it's only a matter of time before she returns, with him close behind. Every woman of the village must make an appearance in his house.

Her father was nowhere to be seen the night he found her walking the trail leading into the village. After weeks of riding alone through the vast, repeating emptiness of the valleys, he saw her come out of the darkness, the braided rope of her hair oiled and swinging. Something lunged in him then, the way mountain lions are known to lunge onto the backs of passing riders. An appetite yanked tight the tendons of his neck and flooded his crotch with blood.

He rode up beside her. "You shouldn't be out here," he said.

She looked at him and quickened her pace. She wasn't even carrying a lantern.

"You shouldn't be out here," he repeated.

"Please, I don't—"

He leapt from his horse and grabbed the rope of her hair, pulling her off the trail. The woman thrashed in the ditch, a flurry of nails and teeth and sand thrown into his eyes. She clawed up at the trail and one of her hands caught the horse's hoof and held it tightly. The man struck her then, on the back of the head. Her hand let go of the hoof and she slipped back into the ditch. He began to strip her naked.

Afterward, he fled back into the valleys, thinking that he'd never return. But the drought already crippling the region continued, until even a day's farm work was impossible to find. Three months of hunger and he gave up, turning his horse once again in the direction of home.

A wave of sand has crested across the back wall of his bedroom. He's tried to sleep against it, but at night the sand inches over his shoulders and gently pours into his lap, so that when he wakes he feels half-fused to the wall, and panics. He climbs into the windowsill and curls up there, brushing the sand from his body. The fear stays, under his skin.

In the morning, the women bring kebabs of horse neck, slathered in fat. Their men bring wooden chairs. They stand on them and string forks up along the house's overhang. The metal catches the sun and scatters shots of light into the house and across his walls. The women in the room shield their faces, as if afraid it would be an omen to be struck in the eyes with that light. He enjoys it. The light is like an excited child running back and forth, room to room. When the wind picks up and the forks strike one another, the sound carries into the hills. The eyes of the women follow after it.

To cook and present the last meal is an honour.

It takes four women to carry in the silver platter normally used for village weddings. They push through sand up to their shins. Sitting in the window, he watches a small white scorpion tap its translucent claws together.

They set the platter down in the sand. The horse's head is pointed upwards, its skin blistered black in some places, cooked tight and brown in most of the others. Its big eyes are a vivid pink the man has only seen in sunsets.

She appears in the doorway, as he knew she would.

"Come and eat," she says, and he sees her face up close in daylight for the first time. Her braid is gone, her hair cut to her jawline. As he climbs out of the window, she looks at his penis, and the beginnings of a sneer pull at her lips.

"There's a berry called a gualat that grows in the Slomah valley south of here. Do you know it?" she asks, sinking onto her knees on the other side of the horse head. Her voice is lower than he expected, her hands older.

"I do."

"I made little slits all along here," she says, pointing to a trail of grooves running along the horse's face, "and I slid gualat berries under the skin before roasting it. The flesh should be tart, a little bitter."

He nods.

"I took out its eyes and lined the sockets with a blend of spices. The eyes I marinated in sugar and wine and put back in only after the roasting. They should be refreshing."

He follows her finger to the horse's lips. They've dried out in the fire and split open. Her finger is trembling.

"I slit the tongue," she says. "Very delicately, I hollowed out the middle and I filled it with peppercorns and slices of lemon, and then I stitched it back together before placing it in the fire."

She stands up and hands him a fork and knife. For a moment he looks at them, and then beyond them, to her belly, where there's a small bump rounding her thin frame.

"Eat," she says. And he does.

It's evening when he pulls the last sour strip of skin from the horse's face and stuffs it into his mouth. The women lift the silver tray and carry the skull out of the house. She is the last to leave, pausing in the doorway.

"I don't deserve such food," he says. "I should be made to eat sand."

"Those flavours are for them, you know," she says, gesturing up into the hills. "They will tear open your belly, and when they do, they'll be pleased with what they find, and think kindly upon my family. You, you're just like the javelina we stuff with sugar apples during the holy days. You're what the children cut through to get at their reward."

At nightfall the children of the village are given a special tea to make them sleep. Their little bodies are then slid under the beds, and their parents join soon after. Even the elders, with their creaking, hardened joints, inch along cold dirt floors to be safely hidden away. Doors are bolted. The village is extinguished, given over to an unbroken darkness. The only sound is the night birds shifting in the branches of the scrubby little trees.

The man stands calf-deep in the sand of his home, watching the lights of the other homes go out one by one. All around him, forks ring and chatter against one another in the dark. He holds his hands together to stop them from shaking.

An hour before dawn, he sees them, at first just shapes in the hills. But then they reveal themselves, and they're nothing like the stories he was raised on. He wants to tell the people of the village how beautiful they are coming down from the hills, that their eyes are swarms of wavering green light, like the fireflies he's seen on his travels in the north. If he doesn't tell them, only the men after him will ever know.

He thinks to call out to the villagers, to her, so that the stories can be told differently to the generations that will follow, but too soon they are climbing over the dunes; they are in the window and through his doorway. The words on his tongue are gone when he goes to speak them. His tongue is gone.

They open his belly, and all her gifts come pouring out.

Hugh Graham

THE MAN

The girls said it was the man. A car accident up the street; chrome and blue sky and a crowd. They said you could see red. The older sister, Karen, went up ahead and the younger one, Wendy, said, "There's blood!" She grabbed my arm and pulled me up the walk. I was yet four then but wanted to go but, yet I was afraid. I tried to see the red under the crowd and the murmur of police radios and the girls kept moving ahead and I was afraid and kept pulling back.

"It's the man!" Karen said.

The girls were five and seven and had a smell of oldness, of having lived: their grey skin, their faded, greyish dresses, their stained teeth, the thick wildness of their hair. They were saying that maybe the man had caused the accident and then I thought the man was lying under the car. They let go and ran on and I followed them, but slowly, because I was afraid that if I went there, they'd take me further into the hot haze and blood and falling darkness and I would be gone forever. Finally I turned and went back down the street to my house.

There were railway tracks up past the street in the distance, and in the weeks that followed I'd hear the trains pass and I'd lie awake, thinking of the accident and the man.

The next time I heard of the man, the girls had taken me all the way up to where the accident had been. They turned and took me along the main street to a corner store and I was afraid of the sun going down. They suddenly became mothers taking me shopping and there was a man called the manager in a white apron staring at them and Karen said, "Hurry, they're closing!" It was because the manager in the apron knew the man and if we were late he would send the man after us. I wanted to go home but Karen had a basket on her arm, her hands hanging with busy self-importance, and she told Wendy to load the basket. The man in the apron watched while the girls counted coins and then he told them to put everything back and they rushed to put it all back, looking for whatever they could pay for. The lights flashed and the man shouted, "Make it snappy," and the lights were going off one by one and we ran out and I thought the man was coming after us and the girls were screaming and pulling me because I couldn't run as fast.

When we were walking and I was out of breath, Wendy pulled five barrettes and three packs of gum from her dress and Karen said, "You shouldn't of. You're going to get it," and Wendy said, "So? They're not going to know."

"The man will find out," Karen said.

"No, he won't," Wendy said. "The man wasn't there."

"The man's gonna kill us. He knows where we live. He knows where Henry lives."

I thought the man would come to get me and I started to cry. The setting sun shone low along the street where the accident had been.

"He doesn't know we were there," Wendy said.

"He lives across the street. He's going to see us," Karen said. "He's a murderer. He killed someone. There was so much blood, it filled up the basement."

I went into my house and my mother said good night to the girls on the porch. As she put me to bed, I tried to tell her about the man but she said it was all right. When I began to sleep there came the sound of the train that ran along in the distance, beside Dupont Street, where the accident had been, in a clacking whisper-roar, a sleeping rush that came as the man suddenly stood up in a brown suit by a washbasin in an attic room lit by a setting sun, red as blood, and there was blood in the basin.

That summer, I played in the moss and clinker and scattered coal by the basement windows of the big old houses; I played under dark sash windows speckled with rain dust, windows that shook when trucks passed and reflected cars at night. Somewhere, as evening came, the man was always in an upper room, under a sloping ceiling, just like my own room, and Wendy said that he slept all day and wakened at sunset, and only then did he wash the blood from his hands.

Wendy and Karen and I and an older girl with glasses called Judy and a sleepy kid called Arthur were on my front lawn and we fell on top of each other, laughing, in a game of Ring Around the Rosie when someone said something about having to be home at dark but then they were on the walk and I went with them around the block to a street I had seen once before and Karen was saying, "He's too little," and though the sun was going down, I didn't want to be too little, so I went with them.

They went far and now I was more afraid to go back alone than to go on with them and the street lights were coming on and they were starting to run ahead of me and I was trying to keep up and not be afraid.

We got to a big street and there were no houses on the other side, just the last of the sky and a twinkling star, and Karen broke into a run, long-legged like a boy, and her legs, then her waist disappeared downward in the dark as if she were being eaten from below by darkness. But it was a hill going down and Karen was ahead and someone said, "Christie Pits." They were gone in windy open darkness and there was a loud bang and sparks and I turned to run and I was jerked back by my arm and Wendy and the others were running, wild, in blowing wind in the dark and there were voices of boys or men and a man in a white shirt and smoke drifting and Karen was there and then was swallowed up and someone yelled, "The man!" and there was hysterical screaming.

Wendy came out of the dark so that I wasn't lost and she said, "Come on!" Karen was screaming to Wendy, "Don't show him! Let's get out of here." They passed a street lamp and a spattering of blood on pavement, red where it pooled, black where it was thin. We were near the edge of the park where the hill went up and Wendy said, "Stay there. Don't move," and pulled down her underpants and peed and stood up flicking up her dress and I saw her vagina, a naked "V" in the pale light as she pulled up her underpants and

Karen yelled at her from a distance, "You stole. I told you." Then they were running up the hill now and my chest was hurting and the man was coming after us to kill us, and I knew I would die because I was behind and couldn't run fast enough.

Wendy ran back and got me and in a while we came to our street and my chest was hurting and my face was wet and I ran in the front door and my mother whacked me on the behind.

Every day I wondered if the man was coming, because Wendy had stolen. Sometimes the man was in the upper room. Sometimes he came down the street, covered with blood from the accident. The man, in his brown suit, could come soundlessly into your house at night and kill you in your sleep. The man was in the western sky. At night, in the dark, I could feel his hands on my neck.

In the fall, when Wendy and Karen were in school, I watched television. I watched *Popeye* and black-and-white seas and an eastern land with minarets and domes and a sky that was grey like the sky outside the window, the sky under which the man slept.

❧

After I started school, my mother took me a few doors up and in through a driveway between two immense walls of houses and into a paved yard where a great elm thrust the concrete into shards and by the back door there was a thin blond boy, younger than I was, playing with a truck under a forsythia bush. My mother introduced him as Stephen and said to stay there until she came back. Stephen looked up at me, frowning, and recited his address: the city, the province, the country.

I asked Stephen if he knew about the man.

"His name is Mr. Gimble," Stephen said.

I extended the road in the dirt for Stephen's truck and said, "The man is a murderer. He murders people."

Stephen stood up and looked to the west and closed one eye in concentration and extended a crooked finger and said, "He comes from over that way."

"The girls across the street said he's coming."

"My parents said not to talk about him," Stephen said. "He used to live here."

"He used to live in your house?"

"I'm not sure. He might live next door."

Stephen's family lived on the top two floors and on the second floor, in the dining room, you could see across the drive and through the neighbours' half-drawn blinds and curtains into big dark rooms where dim figures did things without sound. In Stephen's living room, another window looked sideways to a two-storey veranda and above it you could see the dormer where the girls might have said the man lived. Stephen was pretty sure it was Mr. Gimble. The house was full of a big Ukrainian family, the Dirvitches: the father, the mother, the children, aunts, uncles, a grand-mother and a couple of roomers. My parents had said that roomers were a bad influence and Stephen speculated that they might be murderers. As Stephen's mother was giving us lunch, Stephen said that Mr. Gimble had sneaked down-stairs in the night and carried away Luba Dirvitch's little sister and suffocated her.

"Don't be silly," Stephen's mother said, "Mr. Gimble is running for alderman and he has personal problems and anything you overhear you must not repeat." Whatever that meant, it was only another indication that Mr. Gimble was a danger.

Stephen and I would discuss the problem of Mr. Gimble as we played in my yard or around Stephen's garage. We'd talk about how tall Mr. Gimble was and how quickly he could come. In the corner of my yard, with water from a hose, we dug a hole which would tunnel under continents, eventually trapping Mr. Gimble, and then chase him up through the earth to China which was also west, over the sky, beyond the other side of the block. In the basement of Stephen's house, Stephen turned on his grandfather's radio with its short-wave band and we listened to a shaking carnival sound through static and Stephen said the music came from the land of Mr. Gimble. We fitted some old plumbing through a fruit crate with a funnel for a mouth and an elbow joint for a penis and decided it was Mr. Gimble and poured water through it so that it urinated. This was the potion we kept giving to Mr. Gimble to put him to sleep so we could escape from the basement.

Stephen was always reflecting, calculating. He already knew about numbers. Though he wasn't yet in school, his mother was teaching him to add three and two in pencil on the surface of the enamel table in their kitchen. I didn't see the point of adding three and two.

One Saturday, Stephen and I met Karen and Wendy on the sidewalk and I said, "They know about Mr. Gimble."

"My mother said he's the murderer," Stephen said.

Karen looked at Wendy and said, "Should we tell them?"

"Tell them what?" Karen said.

"That he's the man. All the blood. Over on Euclid Avenue."

Stephen visored his eyes with his hand and frowned at the girls in the sunlight.

"Who's the little guy?" Karen said.

"Stephen."

"Why's he so small?" Wendy said.

"He's my friend," I said.

On the third floor of Stephen's house, on the carpet in his father's study, Stephen and I did a jigsaw puzzle of Zorro in Mexico. I said even Zorro had never found Mr. Gimble and Stephen said that Mr. Gimble had gone through Mexico and I said that the girls had seen Mr. Gimble but Stephen said they were trying to fool me.

Winter came and the girls were gone. They didn't leave, they didn't even move away. They were simply gone. I had never even known where they lived, only that they lived across the street. I remembered their hair, their dresses, their mysterious violence and their stories and secrecy and the infinite profane wonder that lay far back, behind Wendy's grey skin and freckles.

Children whose names I knew, like Arthur and Judy, were gone and so were all the others. My parents said they had moved somewhere called the suburbs.

Stephen and I began to watch television at each other's houses and then one Sunday I was in the third-floor spare room across from his bedroom and through the window onto the alley I saw into the neighbour's window: a room as dark as a fish tank with a strip of burning sunlight on the wall as if a shadow could enter and cross it. I telephoned Stephen and said that Mr. Gimble had moved next door.

Mr. Gimble still wakened and washed his hands and Stephen said that it was time to figure out where he travelled from and returned to. We went outside and copied street signs onto a map. As rain fell in the alley outside the study in my house, we expanded the map to Bathurst and Huron, Bloor to Dupont where the accident had been. The map ended with the train tracks and the escarpment. We marked points on the periphery where Mr. Gimble had been sighted. We added the railway tracks and the Midtown Cinema.

That November, Stephen and I redrew the map, including an enlarged detail with a plan of Stephen's driveway and the garage and the Dirvitch house and when we were out there checking the map, Luba Dirvitch, who was younger, asked what we were doing. We showed her and she said it wasn't allowed and went in and told her mother. Mrs. Dirvitch came outside and Stephen nervously said we were only waiting until his mother came back to give us lunch. Mrs. Dirvitch asked us if we wanted some soup.

The Dirvitches' kitchen was full of steam and the smell of cabbage and as we ate, and Luba watched us suspiciously, we kept glancing down the hall into the darkness which seemed to go on forever and tried to stop laughing about Mr. Gimble. From the Dirvitches' kitchen, Stephen's house, the driveway and the garage and the tree that broke through the concrete looked familiar but unfamiliar: Stephen's house from the other side, skewed and through steam, as if from a different world.

⤬

In September, Stephen was sent to a local grade school and I was sent to a Catholic school that was well to the north, beyond the escarpment, beyond the boundary of the map. On the first day at my school, a lot of the kids in class were talking and the old woman teacher threatened everyone with the strap, and told us if we weren't sorry in our heart we would go to hell and we'd burn. If we'd ever been burned by a cigarette, it would be like that but all over our body and forever.

School loomed above the escarpment, a world of older boys with pointed shoes who smoked cigarettes and greeted each other with a kick to the groin, or Italian girls who already had earrings and breasts, of kids who would knock your hat off to make you hit back so they could beat you up, of teachers who yelled and screamed or made you stand up and ridiculed you. I didn't do as well in school as Stephen did.

When my father was travelling and after the house-keeper left at noon, my mother would sleep for long periods. Sometimes in the evening, when she gave me my dinner, her eyelids would be heavy and she'd tell me I didn't love her. When my father returned, I overheard him arguing with my mother about her drinking.

Sometimes at dinner, when my father was away, my mother would sit staring at me, periodically losing consciousness. There would be no lights on and the sun would be setting and her eyes would open and she'd pick up where she'd left off, telling me that she knew what was going on in my soul and that I hated her, that they were worried about me and were thinking of sending me away. Then she would slump over sideways.

At school, I didn't make friends and always looked forward to getting home, but once home I'd look forward to getting to Stephen's up the street. When I'd mention to Stephen what I'd learned about God and hell, Stephen would have no comment. Stephen seemed to live in a house that was simple and austere in pale light, like the Dutch picture in his living room of a woman in the grey light of a window, the picture itself in the pale light of the window of Stephen's living room.

Stephen's mother had decided he should attend the local Anglican church service and I noticed the jacket and new, awkward-looking brown shoes that Stephen's mother had bought him for Sundays. But in a while it became clear that for Stephen's family, church didn't really matter. In the end, Stephen only went once.

One day, when my mother had passed out and gone to bed, I had dinner at Stephen's and Stephen said that his parents had been talking about moving to Montreal. As I went home that night, the street lights came on and I wondered what would happen when Stephen was gone.

That spring, I was still hoping the move to Montreal would be forgotten when we started writing a play about Mr. Gimble. Mr. Gimble was always somewhere offstage and the characters, a lion, a bear and an elephant, wondered what to do on his approach and the animals had arguments about how to deal with him. The play was called "The Man." In the end, the animals were pursued by Mr. Gimble through mountain and forest and finally caves until the lion and the elephant escaped by deserting the bear. Mr. Gimble tried to kill the bear, but he sank in quicksand and the bear escaped. We didn't find happy endings interesting and we had the bear wander off, wounded and bloody, looking forever for the lion and the elephant.

Stephen was now taller than I was, and thin. Stephen was seven and I was eight but Stephen could already calculate the difference between our weights, multiply it by itself, subtract the weight difference from the product and that would be the height of Mr. Gimble. On weekends now, we wrote a newspaper named for the block. It had its stock page, its news, its women's and sports sections, much of the paper related to Mr. Gimble, all written in columns on lined, legal-sized paper.

Stephen decided that according to the map of the world, Mr. Gimble lived in Rio de Janeiro. I was skeptical and to settle it, we played Pirate and Traveler in Stephen's basement and if either of us landed on Rio de Janeiro, it meant Mr. Gimble was there. I landed on Rio de Janeiro and we argued until we found a compromise. Mr. Gimble was in several places at once. What was more, Mrs. Dirvitch and Mr. Gimble had been lovers and Mrs. Dirvitch had betrayed Mr. Gimble by evicting him and now lived in fear. There was no longer any doubt about Mr. Gimble's other residence when, one Saturday in his basement, Stephen turned the dial of his grandfather's radio and through static on the short-wave band were voices, remote and elegiac, with shaking music. Near the red line on the yellow dial was "Rio de Janeiro."

By Christmas, the bear had staggered, wounded, to Toronto, and Mrs. Dirvitch knew it was only a matter of time before Mr. Gimble would be resurrected from the quicksand outside Rio de Janeiro. The ever-nearing presence had now taken on some urgency and Stephen believed the man, Mr. Gimble, could in theory be located using the stars and he got an astronomy book. Finally, on a map, we drew in the heavens according to the points on the compass. Stephen went into his backyard and squinted at the night sky, again with one eye closed, the same way he had squinted at me when we had first met under the forsythia, the pencil now waving in his thin hand as he slowly marked and erased.

Another year and Stephen's family still hadn't moved. After school now, as the street lights blinked on, Stephen and I played ball hockey with boys from Stephen's school on the broken concrete drive. Sometimes, just the two of us played, opening the garage and making a goal against the back wall with the other goal where the houses narrowed the driveway. When there were enough to make teams, we played fast and violently around the big elm and through crumbled leaves, slapping the ball out of the Dirvitches' wild roses until suppertime when the backs of houses became shadows and the cold was intoxicating, and in the last of the freezing red azure the world was still alive and violent.

∂⋇∂

When the snow had gone and the streets were dirty and damp, Stephen and I went west as far as we could go, into the land where Mr. Gimble had walked. The houses were a little smaller and a lot of the people spoke Italian or other languages and there were more corner stores. It was getting time to turn back when a girl around our age, who was neither white nor black, perhaps a dark Italian or something else, smiled at us chewing gum and asked us, grinning, if we wanted to play games in her basement. We were courteous and asked her what the games were.

"Wait and see," she said, laughing.

We discussed it and Stephen looked at his watch and decided it would be better to get back.

"You don't know what you're missin'," she said. "Prizes and then surprises!" and she laughed.

That spring, after his ninth birthday, Stephen spoke importantly of what he called "my condition," something he called his lymph. I would ask him about it but Stephen wouldn't say much more. Soon Stephen was in bed. In July, Stephen's mother and sister got mad at me and told me not to bother Stephen; he had to rest. In August, I didn't see Stephen at all.

My parents and I brought Stephen puzzles and books in the hospital and I brought the latest edition of the newspaper and its reports on Mr. Gimble, but without Stephen's calculations and geography. On Thanksgiving, at the hospital, Stephen was an odd colour and hardly spoke. In December my parents and I went down to an Anglican funeral home. I was told to stay with my aunt out in the lobby, but through the doors I glimpsed the awkward brown shoes at the end of the coffin; the shoes Stephen had worn only once.

On a clear night in January, I went outside his house and saw the overturned bowl of the firmament, the stars and planets that had their centre above the block, with a planet over Bathurst Street and a constellation over Spadina Road and the shifting skies that tracked the man, ever shifting, but now more distant.

I tried to do another copy of the newspaper but it was difficult. I tried again but I couldn't and I left it. By the study window there was the light of a grey day in the alley, grey like the day we started the play about Mr. Gimble. But I watched television now. I watched it all the time. Sometimes the black-and-white seas in *Popeye* brought the old skies back, the skies of Rio de Janeiro.

One Wednesday I came home from school very tired and barely finished my homework. The following morning

I wakened with my throat sore and my head congested and my mother kept me at home. I had trouble sleeping at night for the heat in my face, and difficulty breathing. In my dreams, the corners of the room would fade into sparkling darkness and the floor would give way into nothing. In the day, I lay in bed and watched television until I had too much trouble breathing. I spent two days in hospital and then my father took me home and now I slept heavily.

I wakened on a Friday, still in the study, and it was raining in the alley and my mother told me they had brought my fever down. Apparently I had nearly died. I got up and moved to the window and saw a glimmer of moss among cracked bricks and the alley was alive with rain. She told me it was April. I dressed and went outside.

The outlines were there, what you saw was there, but everything else was gone. I remembered the sisters, Wendy and Karen, and things came back with the sound of the train that still passed at the end of the street. I remembered Arthur and Judy and faces that had never had names.

I went down Stephen's driveway, past the elm, the broken concrete. By the back door and the forsythia I found Stephen's hockey stick and took shots against the back wall of the garage and Mrs. Dirvitch returned from shopping and asked me if I wanted soup. In the kitchen, there was the steam and the cabbage smell, and then outside, the strangeness of Stephen's house, still there but the other way, distant and backwards. I asked to use the bathroom and Mrs. Dirvitch told me it was upstairs and I went up. I stopped at the door to a big shabby bedroom and saw that it was the mirror image of Stephen's dining room, through the windows. I went in and looked across the alley to Stephen's dining room and like a dream saw myself and Stephen at the table, writing the newspaper.

After I was back at school, I tried to stay away from my parents by watching television or staying in my room or by walking the surrounding streets. One day I went farther west as if I were going off the edge of the earth, all the way west to where Mr. Gimble had been.

These streets had endless pillared porches under a different sky. Someone said "Hi" and I turned and saw the grinning dark girl and she said, "Do you remember me?" She asked me if I wanted some pop and I said okay and she took me down an alley and into a basement rec room and gave me a sickly-sweet cherry soda and turned on a television and introduced me to *American Bandstand*. I mimicked the singers and she doubled up laughing. We had a pushing contest on the sofa and our laughter was drowned by the roar of the train and Mr. Gimble was in the distance and the train receded and she said, teasing, "Will you go steady with me?" A woman yelled from upstairs and footsteps were coming down and the girl told me I had to get out fast and she held out her arms operatically but I just laughed and ran out. I set off for home thinking of her and then turned and tried to remember where her house was. I looked up: Stephen would have said something about it being under Orion, Orion the hunter.

One evening in September, when I'd started Grade 11, my father and mother remarked that Alderman Gimble had gone on trial for using municipal funds to entertain his mistress. Later, I saw him on the news on television: weedy and balding with a pencil moustache and horn-rimmed glasses, waving away reporters.

On a night at home, my mother and father were having coffee and my mother said the bank robber, Bill Gimley, had died in prison. He'd been famed for his sharp brown suits and he'd been living in a rooming house near Christie Pits when it was believed, though never proven, that he'd murdered a suspected informer who was found with his throat cut on the third floor, and in another room there was a basin filled with bloody water. Later, I learned that Wendy and Karen had lived in a basement across the street and that their mother had been a prostitute.

In Grade 11, I liked to pretend I was from nowhere and dress in an anonymous trench coat. After school, I'd get off the bus at a diner, a few blocks from home, and sit and do my homework and read the newspaper while the trains passed, shaking the cereal boxes and rattling the cups. One day in April, I'd just left the diner when I saw the girl coming toward me over the water from the melting snow that ran across the walks. She had a body now and wore a ski jacket. She lived in the same house but this time we went up to the third floor and sat cross-legged on the bed in her room. It was the same game of laughing but soon we were tangled together, half-naked, and there was a noise downstairs and she jumped out of bed, wearing only a sleeveless undershirt and below it the unexpected luxuriance of pubic hair in a band of late sunlight and the train passed, roaring.

It was a long train and I could hear it still going away as I left and I realized I was walking away from home. Dark fell fast and I was in Christie Pits and the wind was wild, the light standards swaying, the pools of light moving in cold abandonment, the wind roaring in the trees and I thought: it's still there, it's all still there, we've been taught in school about things ending and new things beginning. But none of it's true, it's all wrong, it doesn't end. Because I was looking up and Stephen was there among the stars, in the firmament, the whole thing alive and numinous and the great shadow even yet stalking among the houses of the west. And I thought, I know I'll be with that girl again, but I also know Wendy and Karen are there too and even if they're dead they're alive and the fact is, you carry it with you, all of it, as sure as the hunter is fixed, emblazoned in the night sky, as sure as his name is Orion.

Helen Marshall

THE ZHANELL ADLER BRASS SPYGLASS

The Zhanell Adler Brass Spyglass was a masterwork of beauty: the slim brass mailing tube, the swivelling brass mountings and the gleaming mahogany tripod. When Richard Damaske saw it in the catalogue it evoked images of medieval astrolabes and Antikythera mechanisms, seventeenth-century telescopes and Copernican sextants, the abandoned debris of an era of exploration when the world seemed as perfect and new as an egg.

"All right," Richard said, when Danny had finished tearing through the blue-and-silver wrapping paper. "Tonight, Dan-o, tonight we'll get this baby set up and I'll show you something…something that'll just knock your socks off."

"No one says that anymore, Dad."

"Sure, they do, buddy. You still have socks, don't you? Yes? Good. Then be prepared to have them knocked off."

Danny grinned. He was pleased immeasurably by the gift, but pleased also by the way his dad smiled at him. It had been months since his dad had smiled like that.

And so he was almost buoyant with happiness when he nodded off to sleep that night, the Zhanell Adler Brass

Spyglass gleaming in the moonlight like the abandoned relic of some Martian exploration team, and that happiness stayed with him the next morning as he slung his backpack over his shoulders and marched off to North Preparatory Junior Public School. But when Danny came home that evening and he found his dad slumped at their makeshift kitchen table with the morning's newspaper beside him, that feeling wavered.

"Not tonight, okay, Danny?" his dad said, barely looking up. "Can't you see that I'm…it's just. That thing cost a lot of money. God, over five hundred dollars, what was I…And now I have to—" he broke off. "Can you just go play in your room? I'll get you for supper in a little while."

"Sure, Dad," said Danny. "We can do it later. We can do it tomorrow."

But the next day when Danny came home from school he found his dad in the kitchen, shirt soaked into an atlas of water stains. A pipe had burst on the floor above them. The water was beginning to seep through, first in little trickles and then in gushing streams. There was no thought for the Zhanell Adler Brass Spyglass then. Danny spent the evening emptying copper pots and bowls as the ceiling turned the colour of a winter storm blowing in.

"Isn't this fun, Dad?" Danny asked, as he heaved about with a massive soup pot. "We've got to bail faster or else we're going to go under!"

"Damnit, Danny! Just be careful where you put that," his dad replied, and as an afterthought: "Wash your hands! The last thing I need is you getting typhus and your mother breathing down my neck about it; who knows what's in these pipes?"

In the wake of the nautical disaster and the subsequent evenings spent unpacking soggy boxes and blow-drying old clothes, Danny forgot all about the spyglass, but on Friday evening when he trudged through the door, he was surprised to find his dad in his bedroom, the miraculously pristine box folded down and the thing itself pointed out his window, nestled between his fraying, navy curtains.

"Sorry, Dan-o," his dad said. "I know things have been. Different. It's not easy for you. Nor me – ha, but you know that, yeah? But tonight I'm going to knock your socks off just like I promised. Okay, buddy? Even if they don't say that anymore. Tonight is all about you."

"Okay, Dad."

"C'mere." And Danny did, and his dad hugged him in one tight burst of affection before settling him in front of the eyepiece. "Would you look at this? Just look. She's a beauty, isn't she?"

"Sure, Dad," Danny said. "A real beauty."

"You don't get this quality for nothing, not for cheap, no. Not the double-refracting lenses. Not magnifying up to sixty times the naked eye…and, erm, helical focusing rings."

"What's helical focusing rings?"

"Well, helical…like, uh," his dad squinted. "Like a helicopter, you know, but with rings."

Danny smiled. He imagined great spinning blades, he imagined infrared sensors and, and extradimensional something-or-others. "It's great, Dad, really great. Thanks. The best present ever."

At that his dad flushed a deep shade of red that made the faint traces of his beard stand out, and he smiled such a proud, excited smile that Danny couldn't help but grin too.

"Let me show you." His dad adjusted the knobs. "There. Just stand and look into the eyepiece. It should be set up for—"

"Wow!" exclaimed Danny. There it was, the sky awash in a swirl of colours. "What is it?"

"The Orion nebula." Danny's dad frowned. "Is it okay? It says the light pollution makes it hard, you know, but maybe, well, maybe we'll be able to take it out to the field by Papa's place. You'll get some real good images there, I'm guessing."

"A nebula," Danny breathed. "Wow. Is that what it really looks like? Am I really seeing into space?"

His dad chuckled. "Of course, buddy. Well, mostly. That's not what it's like now. It says that everything you're seeing, it's already happened. Something to do with the way light travels. What you're seeing is how it *was*."

"Oh," Danny said.

His dad stumbled, seeming to sense his son's disappointment.

"Don't worry, if we get a really good night, I bet you can see something over a million years old."

"A million years old? Really?"

"I promised I'd show you some really good stuff, didn't I? And here—" His dad picked up something off the bed. "A journal. To record what you see. It's already got your name inside it."

Danny fingered the velvet of the embossed stars and rocket ships before flipping it open. "To Danny Damaske. From Richard Damaske. Lots of love for your twelfth birthday, buddy. Dad."

"Well, you deserve some really good stuff, don't you? A little magic?"

"It *is* magic." Danny wrapped his arms around his dad. "Thanks. Just wait till Evan sees this! It's gonna knock his socks off!"

❧

"I guess it's sort of cool," Evan said. He was reclining on Danny's bed, his arms haphazard, one covering the fringe of bangs his mom couldn't cut quite often enough. "I mean, my dad would never get me something like that."

Evan was in the same grade as him, but his birthday was in February so he had already had a good long time to get used to being twelve. For Danny, twelve was still new. Twelve was still exciting. But for Evan, halfway to thirteen, twelve was already kid stuff.

"It has helical focusing rings," Danny said. "It can magnify up to sixty times the naked eye."

"Huh," Evan allowed.

"It's…"

"It's a bit queer if you ask me. I mean, what do you want with something like that? What does your dad think you are, a queer?"

"What do you mean?" Queer was what they called Pete Cartwright, the new kid from Manchester who had been jumped up a grade.

"I mean, that's why my dad wouldn't get me one. He'd be worried it would make me queer." Evan rolled onto his stomach. The afternoon sun knifed across his face and revealed a landscape of acne craters and freckles.

"You don't want to try it?"

"What for? It's daytime. It's not like there's any planets or anything, except, I mean, for the sun, and that'd just, I dunno, burn your eyeball up like a toasted marshmallow if you looked at it through that thing."

"What about something else? What about…" Danny searched for something definitively not queer. "What about if we look into Sarah Englemont's room?"

The moment the words were out of his mouth it was like someone was turning a radio dial in his head, and what had been a muzzy static of pre-adolescent longing suddenly jumped into sharp relief.

Sarah Englemont.

This was new territory for Danny. He knew some of the other boys from class liked to look at the magazines they sneaked out of Mac's Milk. They all had hiding places – under the bed wasn't good enough, that was a well-known fact. Nor was under the mattress or in the sock drawer. Jammed behind the headboard, taped underneath the dresser, that was better. Sam Stenson, whose parents were both fanatical clean freaks and vacuumed the whole house top to bottom twice a day, had hollowed out an old encyclopedia with a penknife. With all the cleaning, his parents never got around to reading much.

Over the last few months, Danny had watched Evan gain admittance into the secret cadre of boys who had been twelve for some time, sharing their winks and nudges, trading greasy, glossy centrefolds at recess. Sometimes Evan, with a glassy-eyed look, would try to tell Danny about big titties and nipples as round and hard as gumballs. Would tell him about the time he found an inflatable plastic doll with "Bride To Be" Magic-Markered onto its chest discarded behind Spadina Station, and how there had been a hole *down there*, and he was absolutely sure it had been filled with cock slime.

Danny didn't quite get the point of these stories, but sometimes when Evan was done Danny would think about how Mrs. Pembridge's breasts hung like half-filled balloons, and how sometimes when she quizzed them on vocabulary and spelling he might see the beads of sharp, little nipples poking out against her blouse. Then he would feel the same sweaty, glassy look steal over him, and he'd have to keep his workbook over his lap.

The thought came to him again.

Sarah Englemont.

Sarah Englemont was different. Even at twelve, Danny could tell there was a difference. With Mrs. Pembridge you didn't want to feel that way, you didn't want to think about breasts and beady nipples. But Sarah was twenty-six. She used to babysit Danny to help pay for university when his family had lived across the road in the apartment beneath hers. Back in the days when his parents used to do things like "date nights." Back when they could share the same space without wanting to kill one another.

Sarah Englemont was like…she was like the way you felt on a hot August day when the smog and humidity sunk into your skull and made you drowsy. She was like when you ate so much Halloween candy you knew you'd get sick but for just a moment the world was all shimmery. Sarah Englemont was like *that*. Except she wasn't only that. She was…she was…

"Okay," Evan said. Evan didn't know Sarah Englemont, and so could not know the rush of emotion that had flooded Danny's system when he even suggested the possibility of…Like he had stumbled onto something mysterious, like he had wandered into the pharaoh's tomb. "Okay," said Evan, and the glassy look was there so maybe it didn't matter, and Evan understood better than even Danny did. "Show me Sarah Englemont's room."

His bedroom filled up with lazy June sunlight when Danny pulled back the curtains. He looked across the road at 106 Spadina Road where he used to live, he and his dad and his mom all together. And Sarah Englemont in the apartment above, her music leaking through the floorboards at night, the smell of her dinner drifting through the vents, her laughter like a ghost inhabiting the silence his parents never managed to fill.

"There," Danny said.

Lo and behold, *there* was Sarah Englemont's room just above the window that had belonged to his parents' room.

And lo and behold, *there* was Sarah Englemont at the window, curtains open, and – as Evan swung the Zhanell Adler Brass Spyglass in a slow parabola from the sky to 106 Spadina Road – suddenly Danny was sorry he had suggested this. He didn't want to share Sarah Englemont with Evan, not Evan who liked big titties and nipples as round and hard as gumballs, Sarah Englemont wasn't for him, Sarah was his, Sarah was *his*.

But a slow grin was spreading across Evan's face, a sleepy sort of molasses grin that made Danny want to punch him, just land a solid one amidst all those craters and freckles.

"Whoa, Danny, she's a real…she's primo, you know what I'm saying? She's just, yeah. Let's see, baby, let's just see…" Evan pressed his eye against the lens piece so that when Danny turned to look all he could make out was that one red comma eyebrow floating above the mailing tube.

Danny said nothing.

Danny said nothing because Danny had stopped looking at Evan and his molasses-slow grin, his dirty fingers leaving marks like pennies on the polished brass.

Danny was looking at the window where Sarah Englemont lived. Sarah Englemont, who had smiled at him through a shimmer of pink lip gloss, with whom he had watched old black-and-whites like *Casablanca* and *Kind Hearts and Coronets*, and who, when he had struggled with the moving box full of his most prized possessions after his parents split, had given him a look of profound sadness before she ruffled his hair like she used to when he was six even though he was eleven then and never let anyone ruffle his hair.

In that window, by some chance, by fate, by whatever gods watched out for twelve-year-old boys, there was the distant figure of Sarah Englemont. Even from a distance Danny could recognize her McDonald's uniform. He'd seen her in it countless times. She hated the thing, he remembered. She loathed its polyester texture, its awkward cut.

No, Danny thought, no!

Because Sarah Englemont *hated* that uniform. She despised its polyester feel. Its stench of cooked meat and grease, so thoroughly soaked into the thing that not even the laundry machine could strip it out, disgusted her.

No, he wanted to cry out, even as he felt an electric jolt from his balls to his brain. No, don't do that, someone is watching, don't you know someone is watching?

But Sarah Englemont could not hear his silent pleas, and because Sarah Englemont did not know, she proceeded, achingly slowly, to strip off the loathsome uniform.

Her pants first. She removed them easily, slipping out legs that were long and slender. And then the shirt. She began to wiggle. The shirt wouldn't come free. Her head was caught.

Danny was stunned. His breath stalled in his lungs. He couldn't move. He couldn't speak. He was held captive by the scene playing out before him, barely discernible to his naked eye, half-imagined, perhaps, but magnified, perfected and etched in the exquisite detail by all his boy-hood longing. The black lace of her bra. The white strip of flesh above her panties, a strip of white that had he been able to magnify his vision sixtyfold would have revealed a perfect, little bellybutton with a jewelled stud.

Then the shirt was off, and – at last – Danny shook off his paralysis.

"Hey! Don't be such a spaz!" Evan snarled, as an elbow collided painfully with his ribs. The Zhanell Adler Brass Spyglass spiralled wildly and almost clocked Danny a good one in the chin, but then he had it under control, and now *his* eye was pressed to it. He was scanning, madly scanning the windows, found his mom's – he recognized the little floral teapot she kept to hold back the curtains during the day – and brought the scope up a few degrees to find…

"Jesus, what's wrong with you?" Evan grumbled, annoyed. "You can't see anything anyway. She's not even there. What a frigging waste." The older boy rubbed at a spot under his T-shirt. "The thing must be busted. Your dad bought you an old busted-up telescope, how do you like that?" There was bitterness in his voice. As if they had both been let down by his dad's failure. "Who'd want something like that anyway?"

Danny wasn't listening. He had an inkling that he had screwed up, could hear that in Evan's voice, and that he'd pay for it sometime. Even though he and Evan were friends now, something else had entered Evan when he turned twelve. He wasn't a bully. He couldn't be, not yet, not when he was a four-foot-nothing, skinny-assed redhead with a face full of acne, but he *would* be one day and he was already starting to try on the clothes of his older self to see if they might fit.

But Danny didn't care at that moment, though the warning bells were still going off, muted, in the back of his head. He was searching, searching, searching.

Finally, the Zhanell Adler Brass Spyglass slid into place and he knew instinctively that he had found it, that as the image resolved itself he would see something magical and forbidden, whatever Evan said, something that would be worth any number of imaginative future torments.

But as his eye focused, everything looked wrong; it wasn't Sarah Englemont after all. It was an old woman, cigarette clutched between two xanthic-stained, twitching fingers. She let out a smoke plume that curled like a cat's tail out through the open window.

Danny pulled away.

Sarah had tugged on a new, baby-blue cardigan.

Danny looked into the spyglass, but there was only the strange old woman, eyes full of sadness gone stale, chain-smoking through the window.

"I told you, spaz, it's broken. Your dad got you a broken spyglass. What a jerkoff."

◈

That white strip of flesh continued to burn feverishly in Danny's mind even after Evan had left. He masturbated tentatively and then with increasing fervor until he came in a little puff which he wiped away with a tissue.

As his mind went to that sharp, blank place it always went to afterward, it was not the strip of flesh that lingered, but the face of the old woman releasing all that sadness in curls of chalky smoke.

It had been Sarah's room, he was sure of it.

It couldn't have been Sarah's room, he had *seen* Sarah's room and Sarah had been in it, one part of his brain argued. But it *was*, said another more deeply buried part, the reptilian hindbrain that dreamed sex and violence and held that image of Sarah like a mosquito in amber. *It was, it was, you know it was.* The window had the same crumbling ledge, the same paisley, trimmed curtains. Yes, it was the same. Mostly the same. The same, yet different.

∝⁂⌀

"Her name was…Jennifer," Danny's dad said that night at the dinner table. "Something like Jennifer anyway, maybe it was Ginny. Ginny Crowther." He trailed a spoon thoughtfully through the mess of cheese sauce and elbow macaroni clumped in his bowl. It was overcooked to the point that the noodles split easily under the pressure of the spoon. "You wouldn't remember her but she used to watch you sometimes when you were just a baby."

"Was she sad?" Danny asked.

"I guess so. She, uh, passed away about seven years ago. You were, what, five at the time then. You kept asking where she went and if you could see Crowsy again." His dad looked at him oddly. "That's what you called her."

"Did she smoke?"

"Like a chimney," his dad chuckled. "Your mom hated it but I was still smoking then, so she never really said it out loud. But you could tell. Your mom would get this look and she'd never have to say anything, you'd just know immediately that something stuck in her craw." His dad looked away guiltily. "I mean, your mom really loves you, Dan-o. I never want you to think..." He lapsed into silence, and Danny took to dividing the elbow noodles into pulpy confetti.

"Did she..." Danny couldn't think what else to ask.

"I think her husband died in Vietnam or something like that, and then her sons, well, one had a heart attack and when she called to let the other know...he just...the same goddamn thing." He shook his head. "It would make you laugh if it weren't so crazy."

Danny tried to remember her, the smell of cigarettes maybe, how she might have laughed, the colour of her eyes. Crowsy.

His dad blinked, returning to himself. "Not hungry, Danny?"

"Sorry, Dad. It's getting better though. This pot was better."

"Yeah, well, your mom was always the cook. Thanks." Danny's dad stood, and began to clear the dishes away, stacking them in a growing, uneven pile in the sink.

Danny stayed at the table. In his mind he dissected and reassembled the pieces of information his dad had given him. The same window. Two different women, one twenty-six, impossibly perfect. Present. One ancient and grieving, died seven years ago. Past.

Danny thought about the light travelling from distant stars. Whatever you were seeing, it had already happened. It was only the effects that filtered out through the universe, light moving more slowly than time, time moving backwards if you only knew how to look at it properly.

He blinked and caught his dad's shadow falling across where his bowl had been, a tiny ringlet of cheddar-orange left in its place.

"I know it's been hard, but we're okay, right?" His dad's voice was oddly disembodied. "You'd. Well. You'd talk to me if you were having problems." Pause. "Adjusting."

Danny turned and, on an impulse, wrapped his arms around his dad's waist. Richard Damaske's hands lifted and flapped for a moment like startled birds before coming to land on his son's head. He fingered the fine blond hair. To Danny his dad smelled of equal parts stale, chemical nicotine and something sweeter that he couldn't quite recognize – like syrup, maybe. But it didn't matter, it didn't matter because under all that was his dad's smell, and Danny clung to that, breathed it in, let it fill him up.

❧

Every other Tuesday Danny went to his mom's for dinner, and so when Danny came home at the end of the day with his backpack slung over one shoulder, a hand crammed into his side pocket, he walked on the west side of the road rather than the east as he would on every other day of the week. Danny entered the code on the outer door, mumbling the numbers as he did so. He took the elevator up six floors, turned left when the doors slid open and made his way through the overbright corridor. Danny paused in front of Unit 24. He wasn't sure if he was supposed to knock now. He shrugged off his backpack and let it settle in a heap. He waited a moment. Knocked tentatively.

His mom was instantly at the door, thin body etching out an autumn-tree silhouette. "Oh, Danny, you're here. You're here. Good. Perfect. Happy birthday, darling." She kissed him on the cheek. Once. Twice. "Come in! You can put your bag…well, you know what to do, don't you? It's not your first time here."

Danny stepped inside and dragged his bag until it was just inside the door. Green and blue crepe paper stretched like kudzu from corner to corner. A pile of hastily blown balloons rested on the chesterfield.

Danny's mom had dressed for the occasion in a fitted, black wool dress, pearls circling her neck and studding her ears. She was a handsome woman. Had Danny's fine, blond hair and arched eyebrows. But whereas on him they looked slightly feminine, on her they were boyish. Almost androgynous.

"Darling," she said. "Come here, come here. I want you to meet someone."

A slow sinking feeling settled in Danny's stomach.

"This is Henry. Henry Croydon. My friend from work. He's going to join us." As an afterthought: "If that's all right with you. It's your birthday, darling, so if you're not comfortable…"

Henry Croydon emerged from next to the cluster of balloons, and Danny realized they must have been his handiwork. The crepe paper too.

Henry Croydon had bruised bags beneath his eyes. His suit was an identical shade and pattern to the chesterfield. He looked like a high-school vice-principal. Or a small-town crook.'

"Hello, Daniel," Henry Croydon said. "Twelve, eh? That is really something. Congratulations." They shook hands, Danny's sliding in and out with as little contact as possible.

Danny decided he didn't like Henry Croydon. Danny decided he hated Henry Croydon.

"Well," said Danny's mom. She watched the exchange with a kind of sick concentration, and when it was over, she smiled an overdressed smile. "I'm sure my two men will be close as houses."

"Safe as houses," Henry Croydon whispered under his breath, and Danny decided, no, his mom had been right, "safe as houses" didn't make any sense, "safe as houses" was crap.

৺

That night after he had returned to his own apartment across the road, Danny stared through the Zhanell Adler

Brass Spyglass at the bedroom that now belonged to his mom and Henry Croydon, but had once belonged to his mom and his dad. Inside, he could see the floral teapot still holding open the curtains. Beyond it, the queen-sized bed with the chocolate-and-tan duvet his mom had purchased when the building heating had blown out that awful January and the three of them had to curl in all together to keep warm. Danny remembered the feeling of being trapped between two sets of knees and elbows, and every which way he turned there were the wrong angles, but still he had been warm, and his mother had stroked his hair until he slept.

He couldn't remember if his parents had kept that comforter. No, he thought, Henry Croydon would want a new comforter. Henry Croydon wouldn't sleep underneath the same blanket his dad had slept under.

Danny turned the dial on the Zhanell Adler Brass Spyglass. The image went blurry and resolved itself again. The same bedroom, but this time the comforter was askew with a figure half-buried in a mountain of blankets. Sitting on the edge of the bed, a young man with his dad's blunted nose slipped on a slate-grey jacket. Danny watched for a moment longer, and the man in the grey jacket leaned over to pull back the covers. A pale hand emerged first, then a halo of blond hair, then a stomach bulging with the belly-button popped out like a balloon tie.

His mom.

She heaved herself out of the tangle of sheets as if gravity meant something different to her, spine arched, her hand on the small of her back for support, but smiling with a sort of happy, pained smile.

Enough.

Danny turned the dial again, and the image went soft like running watercolours, became a darkened room, curtains pulled shut, backlit by the soft orange glow of the lamp. Cozy. Muted silhouettes behind.

Danny turned the dial.

The same room, curtains pulled back again, a single figure. His dad. Even younger, broad-shouldered with a clean, unlined face that Danny recognized as the one his own might grow into. He was laughing. He looked like a man who laughed often. He was unbuttoning a white dress shirt, the tails pulled out haphazardly at the back to hang in two wrinkled diamonds. He was staring at the doorway.

Danny nudged the Zhanell Adler Brass Spyglass the barest degree. There. The doorway darkened, the light suddenly blinding behind the silhouette of a slim-hipped woman.

She hung in the doorframe for a second that seemed to stretch on and on, husband and son both frozen in time. She was immeasurably beautiful, like a stage performer, otherworldly. The long sheaves of her hair twined into wreathes pinned at the top, the special silk dress she would wear only to the Canadian Opera Company, a Marilyn Monroe dress, black with a net of lace over the shoulders. Father and son stuck in that frame, hung up together on that beautiful woman. Sarah Englemont in ten years. Danny in ten years.

The image held, and then came unstuck. She began to walk from the pooling light of the hallway.

Danny turned the dial back. Found her again, framed in light. Beautiful. Still. She began to move. He reset the image, but he could not get it to stay put, there was no pause button, only an endless slice of time set on repeat. Light filtering out through the universe. Past becoming present.

Danny turned away from the spyglass, taken by the vague shape of some new emotion you must only get after you turned twelve. He tried to think about his mom, but all he could pull up in his mind was the image of the plastic doll with its Magic Marker tattoo. Bride To Be.

He turned back to the spyglass.

When Danny arrived at school Wednesday morning, the Wednesday after his second birthday party, something was different. Off. Like all seventh graders, like all weak creatures in a predatory ecosystem, he had attuned himself to the complex minutiae of his surroundings – the mouths hidden behind cupped hands, the whites of eyeballs rolling away from him, the vicious giggles of Laura G., Laura L., and Laura S., and the immediate hush as he passed them.

These were bad signs.

A kind of hurricane whisper blew across the schoolyard as Danny crossed the twenty yards from the chain-link fence to the doorway. He passed Evan and the other big-tittie boys. Evan smiled casually. His eyebrows had sharpened to points.

Here it is then, Danny thought. The new Evan.

"Hey, Danny." But it wasn't Evan. It was Sam Stenson who spoke, the cauliflower-eared kid next to him with the cut-up encyclopedia and a nose like a faucet. "Hey, Danny boy." It was Sam speaking, but Danny could almost see Evan's mouth moving along.

Time stood still. The storm was breaking around Danny.

"I heard your dad is a queer. I heard your dad likes to…" Sam paused, screwed up his eyes in concentration. His tongue jammed against his cheek, ballooning it in and out.

The trio of Lauras giggled, the giggles spreading out in a fan around them. Danny looked at Evan. Evan looked back at Danny.

"I'm talking to you, Danny boy!" Sam called, rubber-lipped. "And. I heard it's not just men your dad likes. It's. It's. Little boys. He likes to. Watch them." The words were broken up as if Sam was unsure, remembering. The synapses firing too slowly in his brain. But then all at once the words came out in a rush. "That's why your mom kicked him out. Isn't it? Isn't that why you had to move? What I can't figure out is why she kicked you out too. It must've been because you're queer. Are you, Danny? Are you and your dad just a couple of big ole queers?"

The pressure system reversed so quickly Danny could feel his ears popping. And now the silence, the calm, the deadly quiet was all around him, and the hurricane was inside, whipping across his synapses, rattling his teeth.

His fists clenched.

There was a line of drying snot on Sam Stenson's jeans. It caught the morning light like the edge of a knife.

"Don't be such an asshole," Danny wanted to say.

"Everyone knows what your mom really does when she says she's working the night shift," Danny wanted to say.

"Just go to hell," he wanted to say.

Nothing broke that terrible silence.

"No," he wanted to say. "It wasn't him. It was *her*. It was *her*."

"Slut," he wanted to say. "Whore," he wanted to say.

His fingers unclenched.

Sam look at him, glanced at Evan. The silence stretched a moment longer, two, and still there were no words, no punches thrown. The crowd began to stir, restless, making jungle noises.

"Just leave him alone," Evan said at last. "God, Sam, why do you always have to be such a jerk? We all know your mom could suck the chrome off a trailer hitch."

Faint laughter.

"C'mon," Evan said to Danny. "Don't worry about him. I think I heard the bell. We'll be late for class if we don't move."

❧

At home that night Danny sat down to the umpteenth bowl of mac and cheese.

"Did you learn anything interesting today?" Danny's dad asked him.

"No," said Danny.

"Nothing?"

"No."

"Did you want Evan to come over after school tomorrow?"

"No," said Danny.

Silence.

"C'mon, talk to me, buddy. I'm drowning here."

"Why do we always have to eat this stuff for dinner?" Danny asked. "I'm sick of it! It makes me sick, I'm so tired of it! Okay, Dad? Just one night without mac and cheese! Okay?"

Danny realized he was yelling. His dad was staring at him. It hurt Danny to see the pale look of fear flash in his father's eyes, but it also felt good, saying those things out loud, seeing that hurt. Sometimes it felt good to hurt people.

"Okay, buddy," his dad said.

They finished the meal in silence.

❧

Danny hardly looked at the sky anymore.

When Danny put his eye to the spyglass, he kept the notebook his dad had given him beside him. He adjusted the dial methodically, checked the numbers, made a mark with his pencil. Adjusted the dial again.

It was easy once you got the hang of it. No different than what they had been doing in math class, making bar graphs. Charting out the stagger of datasets on grid paper under Mrs. Pembridge's sharp-nippled guidance.

Danny licked his lips. He turned the dial. The window swam into focus. There was the teapot. The brown-and-tan duvet. He waited, but there were no figures in the circle of vision. He tried again, vision blurring and resolving, blurring and resolving. There. His mom standing by the mirror of the dresser, a finger pulling back errant strands of hair behind her ear.

Danny made a note in his book. Turned the dial. Turned the dial again until he found her propped up on pillows with a paperback. She licked her index finger and turned the page. She seemed happy enough, Danny thought, content. He made a note. He turned the dial.

Danny spent the night like this. The next as well. The next after that. He ignored when his dad knocked at the door, learned to turn up the volume on his radio, ate dinner silently, sullenly. Worked. The images went by, smearing across his vision, one superimposed on the next, on the next, on the next. Danny found it strange, captivating, the gradual progression backwards, watching his mom's cheeks smooth out like the skin of an apple until there were only the faintest of lines where the wrinkles would later net at the corner of her eyes and mouth.

Sometimes Danny recorded the moments when she was with his dad, the grey streaks at his temple receding like a tide as the image changed again and again. He was smoking now. Danny watched his arms thicken, his back straighten from its fishhook slump. Danny watched the distance close between them, the way they touched each other, the casual kisses in the morning, the way his dad might run his palms across the side of her face, curving around her ears. The way she would lean into him, sometimes, when she was very tired in the evening.

But mostly Danny watched his mom. Watched the years lift off her, the thick, invisible weight of them peeling off as he turned back the dial click by tiny click.

Slut, he wanted to think. *Whore*, he wanted to think.

But then sometimes there *he* was in the room too. Seven years old. Five years old. Four years old. Vibrating like a puppy, hands in her makeup drawer, interfering, until she would scoop him up underneath his armpits and sit him down on the bed as she got ready for work. Sliding the studs of pearls into her ears. Rouging her cheeks.

Three years old. Two years old. He watched himself shrink smaller and smaller, the mass of him disappearing into thin air. Where am I going? Danny would think. Fingers whittling down to the length of crayons. Of baby carrots. Pudgy baby hands still grasping at the hem of mommy's dress as she swept by him and landed a quick kiss on his forehead.

And then he was the size of a football, and she would keep him swaddled in a blue blanket, torpedo-shaped, legs vanished to a single vertex. They would keep him between them, his mom and his dad, their bodies pressed close but not too close. His dad slept uneasily in those months. Danny would catch him waking in the night, a look on his face like he was afraid he had rolled the wrong way and smothered the little lump of his son.

Smaller and smaller until baby Danny disappeared entirely into her body, and there was just that hot-air-balloon bulge in the stomach and the breasts pillowed above, and then that shrunk too, smoothed over, the mountain becoming a molehill under her navel.

It took Danny nine days to chart out the length of his lifespan. He charted it in smiles. He charted it in touches. He charted it in wrinkles and haircuts and naptimes and workdays.

Slut, he wanted to think. *Mommy*, he wanted to think.

Danny did not watch for his dad. It was that other thing he watched for. Whatever it was that had come between them, that must have started earlier, mustn't it? Something like that couldn't simply arrive without warning. Without being anticipated. Expected.

So Danny watched for it. Watched for Henry Croydon or someone like him. Charted out twelve years back into the past, and then another nine months. He watched for that other thing. He waited for his mom to become the slut he knew she would become.

He watched. It had to be there. Something had to be there.

It wasn't.

❧

"I want to live with Mom," Danny said at the dinner table that night, the hot damp of July having crept into the apartment almost overnight, soaking armpits and crotches with sweat. They were eating Rice-A-Roni mixed with slices of chicken breast.

"What?" his dad asked. He was serving himself a big spoonful from the pot. A glob broke off and landed on the morning newspaper, which had been used as a makeshift placemat. "I want to live with Mom. I want to move back. I don't like it here." *With you*, he wanted to say. *I don't like it here with you.*

"But, Danny. You can't." He paused, stricken. "I mean. Danny, please. We had an agreement. Your mom needs time. We all need some time."

"I can have my old room back," Danny said.

"C'mon, buddy, I know it's been rough here, but it's not that bad, is it? I mean, we're all upset. I know it's not ideal, but I've been trying. Look, I've been trying, you know I've been trying."

"Mom said I could have my room back. Mom said it wouldn't have to be an office if I lived there."

"You can't, Danny. Please. I'll do better, I'll make us something better tomorrow. Chicken fingers, huh? How about that? How about hamburgers and French fries? You love hamburgers and French fries. You can help me in the kitchen, that'd be fun, wouldn't it? Danny?"

"I *hate*," Danny said delicately, "hamburgers and French fries. I hate this apartment. I hate you. I'm going, okay? I'm going."

Before his dad could get up from the table, before he could even stand, Danny was at the door, Danny was slipping on his sneakers, he was in the hallway, he was on the street, he was racing across it and entering the code. He was standing in front of the elevator. The elevator door opened. He stabbed at the button for the seventh floor. The elevator door closed. His heart beat like the wings of a hummingbird in his chest, individual thumps turned to a steady buzz.

Danny listened to the sound of the floor passing, the tinny chime as another one sped beneath him. He imagined his dad at the table, still staring at that stupid spoonful of Rice-A-Roni. Still eating mechanically as if nothing had happened. As if you could simply keep going like nothing had ever happened.

He wondered if he had called his mom. Danny didn't care.

The elevator door slid open and Danny stepped out, turned left and walked through the overbright hallway to Unit 24. He knocked.

He imagined his dad finding the journal. He imagined his dad reading the journal. Wondered if he would understand it.

The door opened. Sarah Englemont's door. Sarah Englemont's apartment.

"Danny," she said. "What are you doing here?"

❧

She was beautiful. She was twenty-six and beautiful, her hair flowing in loose, delicate curls around her shoulders, hair the colour of honey, hair the colour of champagne, skin sweet-smelling, sweet like his dad had smelled.

"You're not supposed to be here, Danny," Sarah Englemont said. "Does your mom know you're here?"

"No," said Danny.

"I can't let you in," she said to him. "Your mom would be so mad, you wouldn't believe it."

"But you have to," Danny said. "Please."

She shifted her weight from foot to foot, but her slender arms continued to block the door. This wasn't right, Danny thought. It wasn't supposed to be like this. She was supposed to let him in. She needed to let him in.

"I can't, little guy. I'm not even supposed to talk to you. I've given notice." She bit her bottom lip, leaving a faint trace of lip gloss on her front teeth. "I'll be out at the end of the month but it took some time to find a new place. Longer than I thought it would. Will you tell your mom that? I didn't mean to talk to you. I'm, just, I'm so sorry, okay?"

Her mouth was curled up into a tight little knot.

"Look, Danny, I have to go, okay? You can't stay here. Just go back downstairs, will you?"

A look came over her face.

"Oh, Christ, Richard. I didn't know he was going to come over. He just showed up."

Danny turned, took in the details of his dad's face in a moment, the flushed skin, the thin slot of his mouth. His eyes were wide.

"It's okay, Sarah," his dad said. His voice was strained, strangled. His hand fit over Danny's, and the skin was hot and dry. "This isn't your fault. Your problem to deal with. I'll take him home." The hand jerked. Danny followed it, only pausing for a moment to look back.

Sarah framed in the doorway, hand smoothing the curl of her hair. The smell of sweetness on the air.

"You can't do that, Danny," his dad said. Angry? Scared? Some other emotion you got when you turned forty? The elevator dropped beneath them and Danny felt his stomach go with it. "You can't run out like that. You can't bother Sarah."

Danny said nothing.

"Please," his dad said. "I'm so sorry, Danny, but please don't talk to her again. Your mom would kill me."

"Why?" Danny asked.

"Because," his dad said, voice quiet, so very, very small. "I'm sorry I did this to you, Danny," he said. "I'm sorry, okay? I didn't mean for it to happen." Then his voice disappeared entirely inside him.

Danny let the world drop away from him, felt it rushing by outside, floor after identical floor.

He looked at his dad. It seemed as if the lines on his face had been drawn on heavy with a Magic Marker. Danny imagined them getting darker and darker, the skin sagging, coming apart in weighted folds. At the eyes first. Around the mouth. Ginny Crowther smoking at the window, the thin plumes breathing out between her lips. His dad's body folding up inside itself, the muscle receding to straw bones, the back hooking and humping, the hair gone grey and brittle as grass.

He had seen it. Danny had seen that. He could look through the Zhanell Adler Brass Spyglass, train it on his dad while he slept, and turn the dial forward. Again. And again. And again. Watch his dad waste away. Watch the wallpaper peel behind him, watch Danny grow up, go away to university, come back once. Twice. A young man. A man growing older. Watch the way he never hugged his father anymore, watch that space between them become a pregnant thing that grew and grew and grew.

"Okay," Danny whispered, child's hand hot in his dad's. "It's okay. Let's go."

K'ari Fisher

SADDLE UP!

My father stopped drinking for one week after the camels arrived. It was my mother's idea to buy them. Sure, my father sold the mules and arranged for their transport, but my mother was the temptress – my father just bit the apple bobbing under his chin. "Look at that!" she had said. "They can walk forty miles a day and can carry two times the amount of one of our mules. It says here that they're called *Ships of the Desert.*" She dragged her finger slowly across the bottom of the lithograph and smiled up at him.

It was that Elliott Shows who gave her the paper: a running advertisement for twenty-five domesticated Bactrian camels with an address from a San Francisco merchant and underneath, a colour lithograph of the first U.S. Camel Brigade. In it a group of smiling young soldiers leading docile camels with guns mounted to their humps. "Look at those heroes," she said softly. "It says here that camels will eat anything."

My mother hated the mules.

It was, possibly, because the mules preferred to eat their bedding hay over her leftover cooking. Or, maybe it was because of my father's unbelievable blindness.

"Mules have heart," he once told me on a rare occasion he was home, as he was showing me how to comb out chiggers without getting kicked in the shins. "Once they're yours, they're yours forever."

Yet, the minute you turned your back, the mules either ran like a crazed horse or kicked you in the head like a donkey. And my mother was right: the mules were finicky. They would only eat uphill on the trail because they didn't like to stretch their necks. They'd refuse their feed until it was laced with sweet corn. And they were so arrogant that they'd only pick one place in the pen to leave a pile of droppings, their favourite place, like a horse stallion.

But they were nothing like stallions.

Even I had to agree with Mom that Dad and his mules paled in comparison to the Stetson-bearing, red-neckerchief-sporting pack horse freighters of the B.C. Pony Express. Dad wore a boiled shirt with mustard armpits and a dusty sombrero tied tight around his neck. He swore its brim kept the rain off his head better than any rodeo flange could.

"Can you imagine it, Chepé?" my mother had said. "The first Cariboo Camels. You'll be like Abraham riding across the desert. See those long, strong legs?" She winked at him.

It was obvious there was much more going on than a simple conversation.

"Look at that, son." My father waved the paper at me, jabbing at it with his stubby finger. "Couldn't you just see me on top of a camel? The mules can only break three miles an hour. I'd like to see the first wolf to come drooling around these beasts only to get kicked in the gums."

I frowned.

The kids were already teasing me about my father. He is one of the shortest men I have ever seen; his clothes are special made by the tailor. The few times I ever saw him without his shirt, I was shocked by the great brown spectacle. My father is savagely furred, with thick arms and a wooden neck. The camels looked swell, but I could only imagine him up there, squat between two wobbling humps. I remained silent and concentrated on slurping down my watery soup.

"Then again, we owe all that money, maybe it's not a good time to make an investment." Mom tapped the table. She shifted her weight and the chair groaned under her.

Money was a sore spot for Dad.

He hardly kept any records and when he did, he wrote in carefully formed Roman numerals. I wasn't sure he really knew how to write actual words. And he'd had a string of bad luck. Last trip he lost two mules to predation and had to pack parts of a steam boiler on his own back. On the first run after spring breakup, a mule packing gold was swept down Snake River never to be found. Plus, Laumeister's mule train only took three months for a return trip and Dad often took four. In many areas the trail was a rough-hewn cliff-side path only wide enough for single-file mules, people on foot, a solitary horse. Sure, gold towns were growing and people were still hiring the Chepé Mule Train – but it was clearly out of necessity. Generally speaking, it wasn't my father who made the hard decisions around home, but the mules were undoubtedly his domain. Dad looked confused. Still, I didn't think he would actually go through with it; everything we owned was made for mules – forty mule-sized trail bridles hung in the tack shed.

"Let's put away this nonsense," my mother said, folding the paper and slipping it into her darning basket where several grey socks lay, wilted and holey.

Last week Mom started mending socks for egg money.

"We could never sell the mules. Why, they're like family. Plus you know nothing about camels," she said, rubbing her fingertips and wincing from invisible pinpricks.

Dad frowned, his bushy eyebrows colliding.

"Woman!" Dad said, taking her fingers to his lips. "Let's not be hasty. At one time I knew nothing about *mules*. Don't you remember when we first met?"

The story is that my father showed up in town ready to gamble, a single man following the gold trail, good with a knife. Then he spent a grand total of one week out on the placer sands, found himself a medium-sized nugget, and bought himself a dozen pack mules and settled in for at least the last ten years.

What my mother had been doing during all this is a little less clear. My mother is dimpled and pale. She doesn't exactly follow the spirit of the other moms who rise before dawn to re-stoke the fire. Yet, when I ask her about what she did before Dad she says, "Being entrepreneurial."

I have never known my father to live a life of anything but everyday routine. He actually whistles when he's out feeding the herd before dawn. The only residuum of any other life that I have ever seen is when he goes to the Boer's to play poker and he rubs a shot of whiskey in his hair like some sort of outlaw. "Whiskey is the world's best hair tonic," he tells me with a slap on the shoulder.

Like he needs hair tonic.

"It's settled then," Mom said. "Oh, Chepé. Everyone will hire a camel train!"

I was shocked.

Dad looked alarmed. Mom reached out and patted his hand. She leaned in close and whispered, "The other day I swear I saw Ezekiel hanging around a pack of gleaners."

Gleaners were the mud-caked kids who spent their days following behind wheelbarrows and picking through discarded mullock heaps for gold flakes. I rolled my eyes in Mother's general direction: that was pushing it too far. Dad peeked at me over his shoulder. I clanked my soupspoon a little harder against the side of my bowl and looked out the kitchen window.

Outside, I could see the mules waiting impatiently for their midday feed. Beyond them was ten acres of green pasture. Sure, it was leased and located right beside the ditch men passed out in after a night at the pub, but we had lived here my entire life. The sycamore tree by the feed shed was perfect for climbing.

Then Dad grinned and playfully slapped Mom across the backside with his sombrero with a familiarity I rarely saw anymore between them.

Mom giggled.

"Woo, Nelly," Dad yodelled, faux-galloping in a tight circle around her like he was suddenly so goddamn excited that he couldn't control himself, like when Pete the John threw his old rag doll up in the air and chased it around. "Saddle Up!"

I was stunned.

Saddle Up! is one of my dad's typical phrases. It would be okay, except that he uses it to mean everything. *Saddle Up!* out of bed Zachariah, it's 4 a.m., we've got to get out to the foal barn; *Saddle Up!* to the mules for a minute while I run into the Stilwell for a shot of whiskey which will actually mean two hours of you waiting by the horse trough; Kids kicked the crap out of you after you stuck up for your hee-haw mule dad, well son, there comes a time when a man just has to *Saddle Up!*; I'm going to spend the next two months out on the trail while that Elliot Shows snickles around your mom, *Saddle Up!* while I'm gone, will you?

All it took was one winter. Dad spent three days drunk in the stable before marching the mules over to Laumeister's. An entire herd of forty mules in full tack is a grandiose sight, but my father at the front looked even smaller than usual. His white shirt, unbuttoned, flapped behind him like a flag. He opened Laumeister's gate. "Ga!" he yelled. They scattered in. More than one tried to kick him in the chest on the way through.

Dad spent the rest of the day at the Stilwell, and when he came home he reached around Mom's waist and slipped a Gold Eagle into her apron pocket. Over Christmas we built a height expansion on the barn and by the time the snow started melting, Dad was no longer the sole owner of a mule train bought with a singular nugget, but in debt to a bunch of businessmen who had never even set foot on the Cariboo Trail.

We have been gone for one week now. Our train consists of Barnard P. Miller, an inventor; Johnny-From-Town, the cook; a modest crew of a half-dozen camel leads; Elfrida Vipont who wants to become a schoolteacher; and twenty-five Bactrian camels.

For the first time, Dad has decided to bring me along. "Imagine," he had said. "The first Cariboo Camels. You and I are going to make history. Saddle Up!"

As if history is something you can ride along on.

Yet for one twinkling moment, I got excited. When the camels first came into our little gateway town, everyone flooded to see the spectacle. The camels are shaggy, two-humped beasts with very impressive lips. Their upper lip is split in two and the halves move independently when they graze, grasping at hay like hairy mittens. They browse the pasture like antelope, always moving. And they seem much harder to offend than the mules ever were.

In the beginning everyone was gushing about the charms of the trail via camel. The camel's thick slipper feet made no noise, and without the clip-clop of 120 iron-shod hooves hitting rocky ground, we were free to listen to the wind sighing in the bush. We wound up impossible cliffs, the smell of sage blooming in our nostrils. The camels carried us high enough to catch the vista beyond the golden-whiskered fields that filled in the rocky slopes along the trail. We raved about how much more weight we were bringing along; how fast we were moving; how much more purple-y the sunset seemed from up high; how well the camels had mastered the science of swimming; how they would eat anything, even the wild spurge that bloated other animals into walking gasbags. The camels seemed perfectly at home in the sandy benchlands. Plus they never needed to be watered; they were happy lip-shovelling bits of snow still thawing at the treeline. I was riding second on the trail and it was hard not to notice how tall Dad was, sitting ahead on the bell mare like he was on a moving throne. He was singing one of those folk songs that I didn't understand the words to, his voice as meaningless and silvery as a bird's. And I thought for one fat second how he had actually done a good thing by buying the camels. I allowed myself to imagine how everyone was going to flock to us for transport and how the B.C. Pony Express was going to go out of business and all the Stetson men were going to come and work for my dad and call *him* boss and he would get them all matching sombreros and the sombrero would be forever more considered the *real cowboy's hat.*

I lingered in that dream until we got to Soda Creek and came face to face with the first horses travelling in the other direction.

Apparently Judge Begbie's team started acting queer miles before they came upon us, their nostrils quivering in confusion. The moment we rounded the bend and his cayuse caught sight of the lead camel, it was all whites-of-the-eye and Begbie bolting through the bush, clinging to his saddle. We spent the rest of the day trying to locate the rest of his team. Dad unsnagged Begbie's cloak from a low tree branch and apologized.

"What were you possibly thinking?" Begbie demanded, shaking his finger in the camel's general direction. He wrote Dad's name on a piece of paper and slipped it into his travelling bible.

After this, Dad started pouring whiskey into his water sack.

I've started spending more time at the back of the train. I am actually beginning to feel a fondness for Lady, my mount. Often I don't have to do anything. Instead, I rest my head on her foremost hump, pillow it under my ear and watch the clouds roll by to somewhere better. The camels walk with a two-legged stride, moving one side before the other, rocking back and forth. It's the type of motion that's easy to sleep to. Barnard is with me at the back. He tells me he's bringing hydraulics to the gold rush, some sort of jet water turbine. He tells me how hydraulic canons blast the gold out of sand cliffs much faster than waiting for a stream to spit it toward a passive sluice box.

"You can't just go out there with a pan and hope a fortune is going to float into it," he says.

Groan. This isn't the first time I've witnessed the fever. The way I see it, these gold men are basically delusional. They hit the trail hoping, with the very meat in their knees, to become rich, but most of them will only make as much money as a San Franciscan peanut peddler. The world these people live in is so slippery that they get all mean and lonely. There's a missing piece inside where their people part should be. What's there instead? A frozen pond, and in the pond a school of suckerfish, sucking at cracks in the ice in a desperate attempt to get to the air on the other side. It's as if they ignored the part about striking it rich being dumb luck. Yes – that's luck that is *dumb*, people. If I end up living the rest of my life in a world where the word "bonanza" elicits a hush in the room, so help me.

We traverse a narrow shelf along the karst landscape of Marble Canyon. In here, even the shadows are hot. The camels start moulting. Every so often we dismount and pull thick odorous carpets from their necks and thighs. We watch as puffs of it sail over the four-thousand-foot cliff only to be picked up by nesting eagles. We are about two miles outside of Pavilion when Sparky falls off the edge.

I was fond of Sparky, an adolescent camel with a penchant for lip hurling. Lip hurling is one of the few playful skills the camels seem to possess, whereby they regurgitate a wad of half-digested grass and use their lower lip like a slingshot to fling green pulpy piles at the bony back-ends of camels ahead in the line. Once, I thought I almost saw

Sparky smile when one of his green wads splatted Phoebe, an exceptionally bony female, right above the tail.

We spend the night in an open cave drilled deep into the rocks while the crew retrieves him. The cliff is about forty feet up to the sky, and somewhere below, past the corkscrew trail, froths the Thompson River. We wouldn't have bothered to get him, probably, if Barnard wasn't so adamant about wanting Sparky's hide for his hydraulic tubing. He was practically drooling over the prospect that camel hide could be a more durable alternative than cow. In the morning he fastens the skin to poles so it doesn't curl while it dries. Then he drapes the entire skin over the side of his mount. He looks outrageously happy as he rides, as if he thinks he is the recipient of some grand prize – like Sparky falling over the cliff was all for him. He looks back at me with a grin and asks if I would like him to make me a playing ball out of the scraps.

We have lived a chain of anxious days. Everybody is irritable and looking for someone to blame. Everybody is looking at my father, blaming him. We've met with three more horse teams and so far all of them went wild with the smell and the sight of the camels. And I'm starting to think that Elfrida Vipont might not be who she says she is.

Last night I saw her coming out of the cook's tent. Every night she spends at least an hour elaborately washing out her bloomers and hanging them from tree branches on the outskirts of camp. Her stockings twinkle like they're impregnated with gold dust. No schoolteacher would wear twinkly stockings. Elfrida is a large woman and her bloomers are impressive. When the wind picks up and momentarily inflates them, I can see at least five whole camels through the leg hole. Even on the trail Elfrida wears dresses with large bustles so her bottom rises out like a shelf, but I suspect it's just accentuating what's already there, underneath, like it's not all window dressing. I'm certain she has strong meaty thighs, like a foaling mare. For someone who wants to be a schoolteacher, she rarely speaks to me, the only youngster. So far, the only encounter we've had was when she told me her name, and then from somewhere in the folds of her massive bearskin coat, fished out a penny candy, dusted off a few shiny black hairs, leaned in, and passed it over.

Criminy. How young does she think I am, anyway?

We've been three weeks on the trail and we are now deep in a hemlock forest. We stop in Spuzzum to pick up a piano. They're paying $1 a pound upon delivery. "Fools," my father says. He straps it onto Bull's back in a makeshift diamond hitch so it rests between his humps and I watch him ignore the fact that it lurches wildly from side to side while he walks.

The path is littered with windfall and movement is slow even on the back of lanky-legged camels. We follow the game trail of deer and goats and come across watering places where springs gush from rocks. It's like we entered a different world where it's dark, moist, and even the air smells like dirt. Brown beard lichens dangle down from branches and the camels sample them endlessly. They spend mornings peeling long strips of bark off the trees with their front teeth, lip-folding it into their mouths where it begins its circular digestive journey. We have to be on guard at all times lest a sailing blob hits us on the back of the head. Their ears twitch even though their faces remain deceptively sleepy. They seem to be enjoying the spongy ground on their feet. They chat to each other, "blo-blo-blo."

Despite the abundance of greenery, last night the camels ate the cook's washing soap and sucked clean his jar of sourdough starter. For breakfast we get nothing but three-day coffee and a hard nail of bread. Johnny-From-Town spits angrily on the ground and rifles through what's left of the food.

Tonight there is a storm coming in as we rush to set up our tents. Dad's acting distant. Dark bags rim the bottom of his eyes. He fiddles for a moment with his sleeping roll and excuses himself to go out to secure the camels. The rain curves the tent in toward me and I can feel how wild it is outside; how we don't belong here. I can sense unseen animals, angry with us, the intruders. The thunder rolls closer, a bass-y bottom to the splitting shot of falling branches. The camels moan like tired dogs and shriek when the thunder strikes. I huddle in my sleeping roll. In the irregular flashes of lightning, I see Elfrida's silhouette through the canvas tent skin, calmly shedding her bearskin coat. Then I watch my father's unmistakable form stumble into her front tent flap.

He's taking long drinks from a bottle. Even over the thrum of rain I can hear her. "K-oh," she clucks, and winds him into her full body with a curve of her arm. She pats his head and leans her pillowy bosom to his ear, her k-oh's spilling out softer, croonier. One of the camels lets out a long, low spine-shivery bellow. *Good Lord deliver us.* I fashion two large lumps out of my canvas roll and plunk my face in the middle.

The next morning we wake up and everything looks the same except brighter and greener, and sometime during the storm the camels ate Elfrida's last pound cake. "Stupid beasts," she says, and looks one of them in the eye with her nostrils flared. The camel continues to chew its soapy regurgitate and I think for one spectacular moment that she might get it right in her gaping hole of a mouth.

We are only a couple of days away from Rocky Ridge when we run into a mail rider. The stallion bucks, and letters and envelopes are tossed into the trees. We stop to help him pick everything up but even as we do, we all know that the camels are doomed. Dad has decided to take an alternate route.

It takes us almost an extra week to get to Wallula Gap, a rugged, frowning canyon, and sit at the edge of a river staring at a narrow Jacob's bridge. It appears to hang almost mid-air, a frail crib work resembling the woven sides of a willow basket. We are now days over schedule. My dad eyes the piano. He steals a sideways glance at Elfrida.

The toothy black slag making up the walls of Wallula Gap is slick with moisture from the churning river fifty feet below. He must see something in my face because he comes over.

"Town's just on the other side of this canyon," he says.

As if I didn't already know it. As if this offers some sort of reassurance. But I can see it in his eyes, the bleary look of hope and desperation. It's the familiar look of convalescence – the one that comes right after gold fever.

It's hard not to notice, in the abundant forest under-growth, how out of place the camels look. They remain dusty brown despite the moist morning dew. Even in the crisp air, they regard the bridge with a heat-enduring indif-ference. They are old world and Muslim conquests in a land that's ripe with new possibilities.

I look down at the frothing river foam at the bottom of the Gap. This is a stupid chance and we all know it. As usual, Dad's mount has eaten around and around the base of her tree until nearly strangling on her gradually shortened rope. She looks over at us expectantly, her cheek flat against the trunk, her eyes bulging.

Dad made his decision months ago and now he can't turn around. He already sold the mules. There's nothing to go back for except Mom, her expectations, an empty tack barn, and a large debt. Lady shifts impatiently beside me.

"Hey, Dad," I say, slapping him on the back. "Saddle Up!"

Dad looks up beneath his sombrero, a large smile on his face. Somehow he has even failed to notice that the camels don't use saddles.

He grabs his mount's reins and patiently untangles her, chastising her gently. One by one the camels step on, the train growing longer and longer, like an uncoiling serpent. The rafters start swinging from side to side with the shifting steps while below the water rushes, picking up alluvium and transporting it to someone standing downstream with a pan in his hands. I shove my face into Lady's hump. It's all dumb luck, I think, and then I hear the clink of Dad's mare's bell as she climbs the bank on the other side.

Linda Rogers

THREE STRIKES

I like baseball. Three strikes and you're out. How clear is that – rules, cut and dried, a perfect covenant, *à la grisette*, Jonathon Swift's poeticized/satirized ho, a piece of jerky in her little grey dress?

> *And, thy beauty thus dispatch'd*
> *Let me praise thy wit unmatched*
> *Set of phrases, cut and dry*
> *Evermore thy tongue supply.*

My mind travels fast, faster than fastballs and agile tongues – from *grisette* to ball(s), ball to diamond, a song "Diamonds Are a Girl's Best Friend," and so on.

The first strike came through the bay window, beveled glass blasted to kingdom come, at least as far as the dining room and, as luck would have it, the kitchen, because the pantry door was open. It was a sunny afternoon. Light leaked in the window and the hole in the window and, of course, it refracted in the lethal bits that penetrated the Martha Stewart wallpaper and slipcovers and the oil painting of his mother, turning his living room into a veritable disco ball.

He never found the ball or the kid who threw or hit the ball, even though he ran directly outside, naked, as it happens, because he had just emerged from the shower, and had a look around. I should say a myopic look, because he hadn't put in his contact lenses. No kid, no ball, no mother dragging kid by the ear to apologize, no contacts. That would be four balls, a walk.

Because he prided himself on logic, he deduced from this lack of forensic information that the beautiful explosion in his living room was caused by a bullet. This is what he told the cops: "I was standing in the window [actually showing his wet/naked/fragrant self to the young Adonis drinking a gin and tonic on his porch across the street] and someone shot at me. Luckily he missed." Did the cop smirk as he wrote this down in his book? Did he roll his eyes when a careful search failed to turn up bullets or balls of any description?

"Were you singing?" the cop asked, a leading question. He apparently wants to be a lawyer and takes every opportunity to practice his clever-in-court theatricals. Windows break when the fat soprano sings.

No runs, no errors. Nothing. The cop left and he was alone with his fears, his undisciplined King Charles spaniel and a sideboard filled with bottles of single malt Scotch. He had a few and then slept like a baby infused with Phenergan.

"It could be car," his cleaning lady, Magda, a Bosnian War survivor, suggested the next morning. "I very scared when car make bang." Magda cleaned up what was left of the glass. ("Oh, Mama in paradise," she said, pulling a glinting sliver out of his mother's right eye, which was appropriate because that is where all of Magda's family now resided, thanks to the sharpshooters in Sarajevo. His mother was probably in hell. He would be willing to bet on that, no prayer on her lips when the drain had been successfully circled).

He agreed, the last thing he needed was to freak out his cleaning lady, who, because of language barriers, didn't realize other cleaning ladies were getting minimum wage, plus carfare, plus lunch.

His dog, who normally thought the world was her big green latrine, refused to go outside and she relieved herself in the bathtub. She also ran and hid under the bed every time the phone rang.

One of those calls was from me. I had ordered a new suit, a bartender and catering for two hundred for the launch party. He was publishing my book on erotic Inuit art, *How to Make Love in a Snowsuit*, and my copy edit was long overdue.

"I can't talk; someone is trying to kill me and my dog is pissing in the bathtub," he said, before hanging up. Translation: the copy edit had met a similar obstruction to the one that made a necessity of daily enemas and prune juice. I decided to cancel the bartender and the catering and wear the Hong Kong suit to a family wedding.

Have you noticed the world is ass over teakettle? We have had four major seismic events in the Ring of Fire over the past year, a hurricane has flattened New York and New

Jersey, a bunch of billionaires have spent trillions on an election that didn't return as much as a loaf of bread, and Barney's in New York is featuring an anorexic size zero five-foot-eleven-inch Minnie Mouse in Jimmy Choo heels and a Vera Wang dress in their *tweeners* display this Christmas.

So who cares if my book comes out? Well, me for one. I spent three freezing years living in igloos, researching sex in sealskins, and polar bears with six legs.

Let me explain. I have in my small collection of aboriginal art a carving of a six-legged polar bear. The sculptor, who was grateful to a missionary for saving his soul and uniting him with his one true love in a Christian marriage, rewarded him with a sculpture of two mating bears. This makes sense. Were we not instructed by the gospels to go forth and multiply? However, the priest rejected the gift, praising the carver's skill but insisting he could not own a piece of pornographic art. The carver, a practical man, took back the sculpture, shaved off the head and forelegs of the male bear, leaving a female with six legs.

Now, doesn't that interesting artifact deserve the attention of the literate public?

Unlike my publisher, I do not have opiate dreams. Mine are of the pragmatic, straight-up archetypal variety. That is, when I am not in too deep a sleep to remember them. After the phone call, I dreamed about polar bears jumping from melting floe to floe, and, come to think of it, whence cometh that particular flow? My dictionary says it is from the Norwegians, who, after they die of cold, are sent out to sea in burning boats. Perhaps someone will send my publisher a burning boat.

And whence cometh the melt? That is another story, perhaps enhanced by my desire for publication, the devil sacrament that uses up the sacred wealth of trees. Pity the polar bears, balancing on shrinking floors, and not a rock in sight. So went my dream, and then I woke up. Perhaps the bay window was penetrated by a rock, and that would also fall into the deliberate column, deliberate but not so dangerous as a bullet.

"Maybe it was a rock," I'd ventured in my next call. "Maybe the guy across the street was offended by your nakedness."

"Not a chance," he said, and went through the list of famous and beautiful men he had slept with. "I've never been rejected."

"How is the edit coming?" I came right out with it. He sighed and I saw my pages melting like ice floes, my book sinking into a cold Arctic sea.

Months passed. I heard that the editor had edited out the most alarming assassination options and accepted the randomness of fate. He had opened his curtains, unlocked his front door and taken his disobedient dog for walks in the urban jungle half a world away from my vanishing tundra and the nuisance grounds that provided me with so much priceless material.

I phoned again. "Can't talk," he said, before putting down the receiver. "I've been traumatized by a home invasion."

His Facebook account reported that a window washer had entered through the door on the second-floor balcony adjoining his bedroom, got into bed and fallen asleep. The editor had arrived home late after an egregious literary event, a book launch (not mine, needless to say), and got between the sheets without taking off his clothes. He assumed the other warm body under the covers was his dog and that was true, but his dog was just one of two warm bodies.

When he called 911, he reported a rape, but the story changed when the same officer who wanted to be a lawyer arrived with his partner, an attractive martial artist called Brenda, who was sleeping with him although both were married to other people. I mention this because it gives a certain *frisson* to the interview. In a subsequent call, my editor reported their conversation.

"You arrived home drunk."

"Yes."

"You took a cab, I assume."

"Uh…"

"I'll be checking."

"Am I the criminal here?"

"You might be. Did you walk the dog?"

"No."

"Wouldn't she have needed to go out?" The cop who wants to be a lawyer was once in the dog unit. He knows how much dogs need *eaties* and *walkies* when their owners arrive home at 10 p.m. after being gone all day.

"I think I told you last time that my dog has been peeing in the bathtub."

"Yes, you did."

"I took off my shoes and fell into bed."

"Then what?"

"I had a dream."

"Yes?"

"I dreamed my dog was dying and I had to give her mouth-to-mouth resuscitation."

"And you woke up kissing your dog on the mouth," Brenda guessed. She was learning vicariously.

"No, it wasn't my dog. It was the man who was in bed with my dog."

"And that man was…?"

"The window washer I hired on my way out the door yesterday morning."

"Then what?"

"Then he raped me."

"How did he do that?"

"The usual way."

"I'm sorry?"

"He penetrated me."

"I thought you were fully dressed."

"I must have undressed in my sleep. I'm a thrasher."

"You thrashed your clothes off, and then the window washer raped you."

"Yes."

The partner of the cop who wanted to be a lawyer lost it at this point and, since she had lost her validity in the interview process, he helped her out to the car. Then they went for coffee.

"They never came back," he told me. "I'm sure he's sleeping with his partner. I heard her tell him she wanted to be in a monotonous relationship."

"When was that?"

"While they were looking under the bed for the window washer."

I am a big admirer of John Irving, who really gets the congruency of sex and death, baseballs in the forehead, penises bitten off during car fellatio. Perhaps my editor has bigger fish to fry, major popular novelist kinds of fish, and this is code for lost. "I have to see a man about a dog." Dogs, to me, à la Vermeer, conjure domestic fidelity, integrity, loyalty, all good things I expect from humans as well as canines. I am confused. Perhaps his dog is also confused. I doubt she's in on it, which constitutes animal cruelty, in my opinion, and my wife agrees with me.

My grandfather used to say that to me about his mysterious disappearances. I didn't know whether he'd gone to the bathroom, gone to make a bet on dogs or horses or gone to get in some putting practice. He certainly didn't mean, "I'm about to get into bed with a man and a dog."

I put my new summer suit in the closet, drank all the champagne (it was the kind with the jar stopper lid and we are going to use the bottles for vinegar, Christmas gifts. I doubt I will send one to my editor, but perhaps I should. Vinegar would be appropriate, but probably too much money to post). My wife, who shared the champagne and the loneliness of the endless nights I'd slept in the igloo a thousand miles away, suggested the shooter/window washer might be another writer. We were now approaching the situation as a shaggy dog story, vaudeville, a Sutra with endless twists. We'd taken to role-playing, changing characters – sometimes I was the male cop, sometimes the window washer, and always my editor. She was always the dog.

We made a joke out of ten years of my life.

I made one last call late in November, tongue ready to either give him a verbal lashing or lick the stamps for the box that held the last bottle of vinegar. He picked up the phone after nine rings and paused. If I weren't the caller and he the callee, I would have hung up. Those pauses never augur well. Most often it is someone in Asia who wants your money. I think he was identifying the number on his phone. I heard him manning up. Then I heard the dog barking. I made note of the timbre so I could encourage my wife to get perfect canine intonation during our next pantomime.

"I was out walking the dog," he said.

"That's good," I said. "So everything's back to normal again."

"N-n-n-no," he answered. "Not at all. I was just shot at in the park."

"Shot at? Are you dead then?" I like the idea of talking to zombies. It has the warm bullshit feel of a Caribbean breeze.

"Yes. No. I was wearing my cashmere coat and it must have stopped the bullets."

"Ah." I wondered if that coat represented my share of his block grant, but pushed that thought back.

"What did it feel like?" I covered the receiver with my hand and told my wife to pick up in the kitchen.

"Like a dull poke."

"A dull poke?" My mind went to the purple vibrator one of my wife's friends used to beat up her unfaithful same-sex partner.

"Maybe it was canes. Were you blocking the sacred path?" I have been to his house. It adjoins a convent, which is now a rest home for elderly nuns.

"That's ridiculous. The nuns adore us."

"Just a thought. She might have left a love offering on the convent lawn. Did you phone the cops?"

"Of course, I went into the public toilet and called them on my cell."

"And?" I was thinking that was dumb. What if he'd been pursued in there, *if* being the big question?

"Nothing. I got the smart-ass cop who wants to be a lawyer."

"And what did he say?"

"Three strikes and you're out."

I could hear my wife snorting in the kitchen. She couldn't help herself. I married her for her uncontrollable laughter.

"That sounds about right."

From now on, I'm going to write fairy tales.

Susan P. Redmayne

BAPTIZED

A spider on the wall above the pantry was looking for a crack in the crown moulding, crawling back and forth along the ceiling line. Rose listened to its tiny footfalls, imagining the little clinging feet crawling through her hair.

The children, as usual, noticed nothing.

The sun had come out, the spring air was warming the yard. In the farmhouse kitchen, Joshua and William were struggling to focus on their math problems. Marjorie and Margaret were underfoot, tugging at their sagging diapers and pawing at Rose's pant legs. The baby fussed from the bassinet. The infant always chortled and cooed like a little angel for his Daddy and for Nana Marie. But when Rose went to pick him up, he stiffening at her touch and spat out his pacifier. She left him alone to cry and kicked the plastic soother with the toe of her slipper. It skittered across the worn linoleum.

"Let's go stretch our legs for a spell," Rose announced.

Her brood scurried for the door. Rose felt plump and slow with the remnants of weight gain from her recent pregnancy. The children tore off down the laneway. Rose was in one of Arthur's old lumberjack coats and had pulled on his muddy rubber boots, too. Her brown hair was stringy and several days past clean. She was glad of the isolation that farm life afforded.

She thought about a meatloaf for dinner. Was there still time to get a pie into the oven? Were the beds made yet? She couldn't believe it was Thursday – or was it already Friday? The days blended together in sameness and routine. She reminded herself of the boys' appointments at the dentist tomorrow. After the embarrassment of forgetting the previous appointments, she knew she had to be more mindful. Or was the appointment next week? So scatterbrained! What they all must think about her in town. In her distraction, she had let the children run off too far ahead. Rose struggled to pull her focus back to the twins who were already making a mess of their clean clothes, splashing in potholes.

"Mind those puddles, now! I won't have you traipsing mud back into my clean house!"

But Rose's eyes were drawn away from the children to an older man who stood unmoving in the shadows of the trees that lined the path running down toward their pond. Though there was distance between them, Rose could tell that he was watching her. He was too old and formally dressed to be one of the country hunters who occasionally stumbled onto their property. The dark colours of his attire and the sharp angles of its tailoring stood out against the soft green growth of the new spring season. His black suit and long wool overcoat accentuated the pale, tissue-like quality of his weathered skin and white hair. He was working his jaw with great exaggerated movements, open and closed and open again, as if exercising muscles that had been clenched shut for some time. But he did not speak.

Rose pulled her husband's coat tighter around her careless outfit. She glanced toward the children and then looked back toward the place where the man had been standing. She stared at the empty space until she convinced herself that she might have imagined him, and then she turned back to the children.

∞✺∞

Some number of days or weeks after that first visitation, Rose could no longer ignore the niggling sensation of being scrutinized from the shadows. If she turned quickly to look over her shoulder, sometimes she thought she caught a flash of black coattails disappearing behind a tree trunk. It was often no more than a smudge of darkness against the glorious summer backdrop, but it could no longer be dismissed.

"Why do you do that?" Her husband had caught her spinning quickly on her heels as she walked up the porch steps.

"Do what, Arthur?"

"You're constantly looking over your shoulder."

"Someone is watching us, I think. All the time. Watching me, and sometimes you, too, and the children."

"Are you sure you aren't imagining things, again? I don't see anyone."

"He's not here now."

"Sounds a bit silly."

"I've been seeing someone."

"Here? On our farm?"

"Skulking near the pond. Or around the barn. He wears dark clothes."

"Rose, honey, it's probably just one of the Wright boys doing some fishing."

"It's not one of the Wright boys, Arthur. It's not a boy at all."

Arthur yanked open the screen door and disappeared into the gloomy interior of the house. The door recoiled on its springs and slammed shut in front of her. *Strangers are everywhere*, Rose thought.

❧

"Are you lost? This is a private property."

Rose had caught the old man peering at her from behind the hedgerow surrounding her vegetable garden. With the wave of a wrinkled hand in a tip-of-the-hat flourish, he bowed and cleared his throat.

"No, my dear madam. Not lost. Not lost at all! I am Brother Ambrose, and I am very pleased to meet you at last. Very pleased."

His voice was higher pitched than she expected from a man, even one as old as he was, and yet it reverberated around the yard. The children, who were playing nearby, took no notice of him.

"Well, then, Mr. Ambrose, I'm afraid I'm… "

"*Brother* Ambrose, my dear lady."

"Yes, well, the laneway here will take you back to the main road. As you can see, I'm quite busy, just now, so I'm afraid you'll have to excuse me." Rose wiped her muddy hands against her pant legs, leaving streaks of dirt across the fabric.

"Oh yes, I see. What a brood! Given your husband quite a quiverful. He won't be shorthanded if he meets with enemies at the gate! Not shorthanded at all!"

"Are you from a church, Brother Ambrose?"

"No, madam! From no church. Not from a church, no! I preach, I suppose, but not from a pulpit. I'm more of a wanderer." He hopped nimbly over the row of lettuce plants toward her.

"Oh. I ask because of your name, of course. And I recognized the psalm, about the quiver of arrows and the enemies at the gate. The one about receiving the blessing of children, as frequently as God allows. I love that passage. My husband and I have been very blessed, as you can see."

"Blessed four times already, I see!" He turned to the children who were stomping in puddles.

"No, Brother Ambrose. Five times blessed, if you count the baby."

"There's a baby?"

Rose had left Christopher in his bassinet back at the house, hoping the infant would bawl himself to sleep. She chewed at a hangnail until it started to bleed.

"Tsk, tsk. Forgot the baby, did you? Bad mommy!" Brother Ambrose waggled a disapproving finger. "The children, the poor children!"

"You're here about my children?" Rose raised a hand to her throat. Brother Ambrose crept forward, looming so close she could smell his mildewy breath. She took a step backwards, almost tripping herself.

"Please excuse me, I should run back to the house. It seems I've left Christopher behind. How mindless of me! I think I hear him crying."

"Is your husband at home, madam? Perhaps I should speak to him. You've gone rather pale. Quite pale. Perhaps you need to sit while I speak with your husband, alone."

"Arthur's not home."

"More's the pity. Gone whoring about town, has he? Leaving you stuck here with his dirty brats? What a shame you opened your womb to a whoremonger."

Brother Ambrose spoke as softly as silk bandages being wrapped around open wounds.

"What are you talking about?" Rose twisted at a clump of her hair, yanking at it until her scalp hurt.

"Now, now, there is no call for that tone. No call! I'm here to help. Just to help."

"With what?"

Brother Ambrose sighed and shook his head. "The children! To help with the children!"

He raised his hands and pressed his palms against her temples. Images flickered through her mind, like billboards whizzing by. Her husband in bed with other women, two or three at a time, all laughing together. The ladies at the church pretending to be friendly, yet mocking her behind their hymnals. The lacy curtains in the houses around town pulled shut, hiding slick, sweaty bodies writhing, fornicating. And worst of all, the Sunday school room filled with children who looked like her own brood but belonged to other mothers, all from Arthur's seed!

"It's not true! It can't be true!"

"Listen to me, Rose. Pay attention. I have a message for you. Hear the Word!" His arms were now outstretched toward the sky. "Your children need to be saved! You need to show them God's grace!"

"Saved from what?"

"They are not righteous. Their mother laid with a whoremonger and soiled her loins. Liberate them from sin! Sin! The sins of the father!"

Rose heard his jawbone unhinge and then click back into place.

"Come for a walk with me, Rosey, down to the pond. Let's talk for a spell about what needs to be done to save you all from ruination! And damnation!"

❧

Arthur held the leather-bound photo album open, spread across their laps. The pages were made from stiff, black paper and each photograph was held in place with gold foil corners.

"Look how pretty you were, Rose. And young."

He was pointing to the first portrait, taken just before she'd left for the church, in the living room of Rose's parents' home.

"Remember how hot it was?"

She felt sodden – a side effect of the new medication. Hallucinations. All the fancy words the doctor used about her disordered thinking, her disruptions in the household. Her arms felt heavy so she rested her hands, folded and still, in her lap under the heavy book. Arthur dabbed at a corner of Rose's mouth with a tissue balled up in his hand.

"Remember the grasshoppers, how they got caught up in the lace of your skirt?"

Rose remembered her innocence, how she had saved herself until that day, giving herself to her husband. Trusting him.

"Here we are standing at the altar, saying our vows. That was the best day of our lives, Rose. The best day."

Rose recalled how the headlamps bounced and lit the way as they drove their truck down the gravel lane to the farmhouse. Their little white farmhouse. Giddy from wine. Arthur's fingertips on the pearl buttons that ran down the back of her wedding dress. The mounds of tulle and lace on the floorboards of their bedroom.

"We're going to be happy again, Rose. You'll see. You're just a little tired from the baby. We'll get you home and everything will be right as rain."

Back to her children. *Yes.*

"Nana Marie is going to stay for a spell. Until you get back on your feet, back to feeling like your old self."

Rose had a feeling that her old self was gone for good. Black pages were flipped. Rose stared at a brownish water stain on one of the ceiling tiles above them. A leak, concealed. Rose thought she could smell the black mould that festered on the other side. Rotting and wild like the decay in the choked-off pond at the rear of their property.

"I think the doctor would like to see you stay for a few more days, but won't home feel nice? That's what I told the doctor. Your own bed! Our bed, all clean and nice."

Rose sighed, eyes wandering to the window that overlooked the courtyard at the hospital. The trees outside must be filled with birds, Rose thought, though she could hear nothing of them through the panes of the window painted shut, dead white. Arthur reached across and grabbed Rose's chin, jerking her head back to face him.

"Don't you be rude and look away when I'm talking. Stay focused, Rose. Stay focused on me when I'm talking to you."

❧

Rose tried harder. When they got back to the farm, and the older children rushed out to meet her at the car door, Rose almost fooled herself with her smiles and open arms. *We must look like one of those happy families in a store-bought picture frame.* It would take vigilance to hide the darkness that had taken hold of her, a darkness that the medication only dulled. *Be pleasant and focus, Rose*, she told herself.

❧

As she washed up from breakfast one day, Rose saw Brother Ambrose leaning against the gate to the orchard, staring at her older boys who were supposed to be picking apples. Their small sneakered feet pounded the hardened earth, branches heavy with autumn fruit whispered against the sleeves of their windbreakers. Brother Ambrose's face darkened with what seemed like disgust.

"You wayward, rebellious boys! Disobedient, uncouth, ill-mannered delinquents! Rose! Rose! Don't you ever look at what they're doing? Don't you care?"

The boys continued with their game, unmoved by the scolding, indifferent to the old man. Rose wiped her hands on her apron and sighed.

Nana Marie, Rose's mother-in-law, looked up from her mending. She'd settled herself into the spare bedroom during Rose's hospital stay. She was a large woman with a loud voice and a cackling laugh.

"What is it, Rose?"

"The boys. They've made a mess out back. Apples everywhere."

"Oh, well. Boys'll be boys, I suppose!"

Nana Marie's loose-fitting cotton blouse was unbuttoned to the cleavage between her sagging breasts. Rose imagined her husband as a baby, latched there, pulling and sucking. It sickened her. Rose shuddered to think that her own babies had clasped those same nipples when Rose was away, Nana Marie's sour milk force-fed into their pink mouths.

"You've come unfastened, Nana Marie."

"These buttons just won't stay done up!"

"Arthur wouldn't like it."

"It's nothing our Arthur hasn't seen before." Nana Marie made no move to fix her shirt. She went back to her mending.

꧁꧂

The forked tails of the barn swallows looked like serpent tongues. Fading afternoon sunlight filtered into the hayloft through the rippled glass of old windows. The flapping wings stirred up swirls of dust motes. Rose lay on her back among the hay bales, listening to the birds. Some heckled, others dove at her head. Brother Ambrose let the barn swallows chastise her for a spell. He laughed and danced, his long limbs flapped, his hard-soled shoes thumped against the floorboards. He raised his open palms to the roof to encourage a boisterous crescendo among the birds. And then, with a clenching of his fists, all noise ceased except for the creaks and groans of the old barn as the wind gusted outside.

"My dear Rose. Swallows in the rafters, cow's milk for ever after!"

"Arthur will be wondering where I am."

"If that man were concerned about you, we wouldn't be in this mess!"

"Don't speak ill of my husband. Please."

"Don't please me. Please the Lord. Please Him through the sacrament of baptism."

"They've been christened. All five. At our church."

Rose was on her feet now.

"Don't you walk away from me, Rose. Don't you dare!"

Rose stopped.

"That baptismal font was impure! Did you see the water blessed? Did you see it with your own eyes?"

"Our minister is a good man. We trust him."

"Trust *him*? Him, of all people? That wretched man who comes slithering around here, insinuating himself. You disappoint me, Rose. You disappoint the Lord above. The unclean will not be received. Hear the Word. Your boys, Joshua and William. The twins, Marjorie and Margaret."

"I'm a good mother."

"Are you *really*? What about Christopher! Toddling now, isn't he? What a wayward brood, defying you at every turn. Lost, lost. All of them lost."

❧

Nana Marie was peeking through the farmhouse curtains as Rose appeared in the laneway, rushing from the barn.

"Here she comes now."

"I told you, old woman," Arthur said, not looking up from his newspaper. "Rose always comes back. Don't let her see you watching out for her. You know that upsets her."

"She didn't see me, don't you worry. Help me get the children to the table. I'll start dishing up the stew."

"Kids," Arthur called.

"Arthur, please just go and round your brood up. It's like having six children in this house instead of five."

"That's my food you're cooking, in my kitchen. You show me respect."

"Getting babies on that poor woman, even after the doctor said no more."

"No doctor is going to counsel me to thwart what the Bible teaches. That would be like inviting the devil in when he comes knocking at the door. God will not bestow more than we can handle, praise Him."

Nana Marie flashed her eyes. "Devil's on the doorstep, Arthur. Knock, knock."

❧

When Rose came in, Nana Marie was humming to herself and ladling stew into soup bowls from a cast-iron pot on the stovetop. Everyone looked up from what they were doing to stare at her. Caught in the act.

"It's pill time, dear. Let me bring you a glass of water," Nana Marie said. "Be a good girl. Swallow them down, and eat up while the stew's hot."

"I was thinking I'd stop taking them. I've been feeling so good."

"Don't be silly, child. You heard what the doctor said. You aren't going to get well overnight."

"But I don't like the way they make me feel. It makes it hard to take care of things around the house. I can't think clearly."

"Arthur, talk to your wife…"

"It's up to Rose. Maybe it's time for her to stop. Get back to her old self. She was just a bit tired from the baby, that's all. Sometimes you just have to force things to get back to normal."

The twins were staring at their mother, eyes wide, spoons poised over their bowls of beef and vegetables, their round faces smudged with grime.

"Marjorie, Margaret. Look at the two of you. You're both a mess. You should have washed those faces and hands before coming to supper."

The twins looked at Rose, saying nothing.

"I'll give them their baths after supper, Rose. The boys, too. Don't worry about it just now. Let's all of us just eat in peace."

"Well, I think they should wash up now."

"And I think you should let them eat while it's hot. A little dirt never hurt no one. Arthur, don't you agree? Arthur?"

Arthur ate his stew from behind his newspaper. Nana Marie threw up her hands. Rose smirked.

❧

There was a dead bird on the floor of the barn, its neck limp and angled, its wings slack and legs folded back against its belly. Newly dead.

"Joshua! My God! What have you done?"

Rose had caught Joshua and William throwing rocks at the swallows' nests, trying to make the little muddy cups fall to the floor so they could stomp on them, crush them. She yanked her oldest child's arm, spinning him to face her. She pressed her palms to his round cheeks to hold his head in place, to compel his attention.

"God is watching you, boy. Don't you feel His eyes on you? Chickens don't lay if the swallows fly away! That what you want? For all of us to suffer?"

"The bird was dead. It wasn't me!"

"We've got to ask God's forgiveness!"

William stood with his thumb in his mouth.

"I want Daddy." Joshua twisted out of Rose's grasp. "I want Nana Marie! You're hurting me!"

He ran from her without looking back.

William did not move.

Rose inspected the fallen nests, the carcass with the broken neck. Most of the barn swallows, the birds that had served as the consolers of Christ on the cross, had long ago abandoned their nests. No one could remember when there had been so few birds in the barn. But the echo of their chirps had not yet faded in Rose's mind. She would always remember. These were the signs that Brother Ambrose had told her to watch for.

Rose heard the *swoosh* of his overcoat behind her, Brother Ambrose whirling and dancing in the shadows. But when she turned to look back, there was only the dank lingering scent of something stale in the air. Taking hold of William, she strode toward the door.

Nana Marie had gone to town for groceries. Arthur was hard at milking and other chores. Arthur thought that Rose having time alone with the children would renew her sense of responsibility, renew her purpose. Rose tried to settle the children to their home-schooling lessons at the kitchen table but Brother Ambrose was pacing back and forth behind her, muttering condemnations under his breath.

"Rosey, Rosey, Rosey."

Rose bent over Joshua to check his sums.

"Your son is lustful! Be mindful! Watch his eyes, watch how he watches you when you bend over him! Watch how he watches his sisters! The sins of the father, the sins of the father!"

Rose tried to focus on the children.

"Such lustful intent. Joshua has already sinned with his sisters. That boy is a sinner in his heart of hearts. A sinner and a liar. You know I speak the truth, Rose."

Joshua, William, Marjorie and Margaret were all seated at the table. Small Christopher was playing cymbals with pots and lids on the floor. Rose inhaled. They stunk of the well water they had been bathed in. They reeked of the Ivory soap that floated in the tub and the dollar-store baby shampoo that Nana Marie insisted on buying to save money. There was a stench about them of mildewy towels from the linen cupboard. Rose used to like the smell of her babies. Now they smelled of having wallowed with each other.

"Your young ones can't keep their way pure, Rose. Their small minds being so set upon the flesh, they will not inherit the kingdom of the Lord!"

Rose put her hands to her ears.

"There is such wickedness among you. It shall be as scripture says, they have wrought confusion. If you do nothing, blood will be on your hands."

❧

When she lay in bed that night, awaiting sleep, her mind a whirling disarray of anxious thoughts, she heard the clicking of his jaw from the darkness. She could hear the creaking of floorboards as he paced back and forth in front of the children's bedroom doors. She could make out his shadow in the hallway outside her own door. He shook his head in disappointment. *Rosey Posey.* It was time to be resolved in her actions and to move forward.

Lucky for Rose, they couldn't watch her all the time. Nana Marie always said good night early before she retired to her room at the back of the house, and Arthur could be counted upon to fall into a sound sleep when his belly was full from a Saturday roast dinner. Arthur didn't stir when the hinges squeaked on the old bedroom door. No one awoke when the treads on the staircase groaned under her bare feet. Rose went up and down the stairs five times that night. Except for the eldest boy, the most willful of the bunch, who tried to pull his hand from hers at the edge of the pond, who almost got away from her, each one of the children had gone with her without a struggle, one by one, still wearing their white nightshirts. Brother Ambrose watched from the far shore, arms outstretched in voiceless prayer.

❧

Nana Marie found Rose in the kitchen in the morning, the hem of her nightgown still wet, muddy footprints on the faded linoleum. She sat at the kitchen table, a serene expression on her face. There had been leeches in the stagnant shallows at the edge of the pond, leeches that clung to Rose's bare legs, grown fat and black as they'd suckled against her skin. Rose had picked at some of them, and they had detached easily, satiated. There were trails of blood dripping down Rose's shins from where they had latched onto her. The other leeches left in place clung like dark scars to the fair skin of her shins.

"Rose! My God! What have you been up to?"

"Do you know what time it is, Nana Marie?"

"Have you been walking at the water's edge?"

"I asked you if you know what time it is."

"We need to get you cleaned up."

"I think you'd best get Arthur out of his bed. He's still snoring away. It was time, time, time. Long past the time."

"Dear, I'm afraid. What time is it?"

"Time to wash them clean. In the blood of the Lamb. Pure."

She laughed, more than confident, almost brazenly, certain of herself, and she laughed again as she pointed at the confusion on her mother-in-law's face.

Matthew R. Loney

THE PIGEONS
OF PESHAWAR

SUNRISE – 6:44 AM

Men wrapped in shawls weave bicycles through oncoming
streams of rickshaws. Two-pitched car horns startle the spit
from mules. Wagons of bricks rumble past, emphatic and
wrestling along the road's pocked pavement. Gathered at
their motorbikes, gangs of Sikh men yawn and toy beneath
their fingernails, awakening in the diesel-fumed dawn.
Against the wall of Lahore station – a lingering sand-brick
fortress of British Imperialism parked on Pakistan's eastern
border with India – the roadside swells in front of my plastic stool as the barber leans in. From the mosque's turret, a
black compass point against the haze of the Punjabi plains,
the muezzin sirens out the call to prayer: The holy moans of
Islam coat the waking city.

—No turning – his chestnut hand steadies my brow –
You want to save your head? Still, still.

As his razor scrapes my jaw, the cologne of his wrist
lands in my nostrils – spiced aftershave mixed with the
sweat of his undershirt. His eyes are yellowed, their corners

faintly bloodshot; his ebony moustache is coarse and blunt as a broom. Leaning to the barbers next to him, he exhibits the blade he's drawn. Men in coloured shalwars peer in from behind: Semi-circular, hands hooked, they are curious and indolent at the sight of me, my whiskers, the strangeness of my downhill skis propped against the station's wall. Their notes of Urdu laughter perch on my shoulders as they study the blond stubble littering the heap of foam.

—Gold beard – he wipes the razor on a scrap of cloth and brings it again to my lip.

Here is that alien bewilderment, that deeper paralysis of difference. Here the history fields still vibrate in their aftermath like the heartbeat of a bomb. It is right to have come, I affirm, wading through this strangeness alone while Adrian is still farther, still ahead of me, settled in a guesthouse somewhere high in the Karakoram. We are ten years older and have let the drift of our lives separate us like an ice floe. Our purpose for coming, we reasoned and planned weeks earlier via email, was that once on our skis again, we might finally outrun what had chased us since high school.

—Finished – the barber blots me with a corner of newsprint – Beautiful as a boy.

—*Shukria* – I say. Thank you.

—You are leaving Lahore? – he inquires – Today? So soon?

—This evening's train. Lahore to Islamabad and then Gilgit to Karakoram.

—Gilgit? – he worries his eyebrows – *Inshallah,* you will be safe. They are proud to be bandits there. Lacking shame!

Some birds eat fruit and other birds eat flesh. I pray you encounter only those with beaks made for berries.

—*Inshallah* – I hand him a five-rupee note, take my skis and pass between the stares of the shalwar men back into the flutter of the station.

The interior hall is a carnival of travellers, the Pakistani railways churning at full throttle. Turbaned porters ferry sacks of onions and firewood; ticket vendors holler their destinations from speakers wired near the ceiling fans. Like a belt, this station is Pakistan's buckle to the subcontinent, a suture to the severed shore of the Indian wound.

After an overnight train from Delhi I arrived in Lahore before dawn. Crossing the border in the dark, my carriage was a party of celebrating Sikh pilgrims. I couldn't sleep for the heat and noise so I lay on the mid-tier bunk, rocking, staring out the window at the passing countryside. Moonlit palm trees laid indigo shadows onto the fields. The unfamiliar constellations of this hemisphere rotated in the black sky beyond them. I watched as a man on horseback galloped beside the train, the moonlight carving between the animal's hooves as it ran. I could have sworn the rider caught my eye and grinned as he rode, his teeth gleaming in the milky light. Hunched forward, he galloped faster. I felt drenched in the adrenaline of far, of utter distance, as though I had reached the foggiest corner of the planet that still held some perfect secret, where it was all sights and sounds altered from what I knew or could imagine. Here, the unparallel life-fringed border to the ribbon of travel – roadsides, tracksides, hillsides, waysides. The world, I assure myself, is full of birds that eat berries.

Adrian and I had arranged for our guide to the glacier, a local man named Akram, to meet my train, and although there'd been an email from him the previous day confirming my arrival, he hadn't been at the station like he promised. Without a way to get in contact, I resigned to wait out the day alone. I found a cart selling naan and dhal and then paid for a shave with the roadside barber. Now against the wall of the central platform as the sun transforms the city from indigo to orange, I find a clean-swept corner to lay my backpack and skis and wait for him. I'll watch for him here and if he never shows, I'll take the train to Islamabad myself. After ten years, face to face with Adrian tonight, I have imagined shaking his hand a thousand times. Adrian, who had frozen some object inside me that had broken off and begun travelling my coasts like an iceberg.

DHUHR – 11:52 AM

—Shane, buddy! – Adrian's webcam image stammered in low-res with the poor connection. Behind him the streets of Islamabad ignited my laptop's screen – Are you really coming?

—Got the skis waxed already.

—Man, you've never seen anything like this place. It's something real, that's for sure.

—I think I just saw a herd of goats pass behind you. Yeah, I'm coming. Of course I am. You sure those hills are worth the trip?

—Hills? My God, Shane, these aren't hills. They're goddamn monsters. But we're skiing glaciers this time. Biafo, right? She's got K2 in the background and the largest run of pristine snow outside the poles. You up for it? I know you remember some of the tricks I taught you in practice. Monsters, buddy. Nasty goddamn ghouls.

The Biafo Glacier, a powder-topped tongue of frozen till edged by mile-deep crevasses. Tucked in a forsaken notch of Pakistan, the glacier creeps between the Karakoram, the icy foothills of the Himalayas, inch by inch toward the ocean.

—You sure you can make it here alone? I've told the guys all about you and our crazy times on ski team. Did you know no one else keeps in touch with their mates from high school? Is that weird or what?

—I'll be coming a few weeks early to see the sights in Delhi so I'll meet you in Gilgit.

—Man, this place is the real deal, I'm telling you. Those runs we did for team were a driveway compared to these.

The image of Adrian turned in a sweep of pixels as a group of women clad in burkas entered the café behind him, their curtains of fabric disguising them like bandits caught on security camera.

—Those the goats you were talking about? – Adrian turned back to the screen, all teeth in the webcam – I'm telling you, Shane, it's the dark side of the moon here. You'll love it. I'll send Akram to meet you wherever you want.

Lahore's a fun town. Take the train from Delhi and meet him there. He's the son of two rich Pakis but British as they come. You'll see, Shane, he's hysterical.

—It'll be great to see you.

—No kidding, buddy. Ten years go by in a flash.

Ten years since high school, since the ski team with Adrian when we rode to the top of the slope together, our feet dangling above the tree caps. From the chair behind us Mr. Mason called out – *Boys, I want to see you work the fall line directly as possible. Got it? Carve tight off the front trough while keeping your pace constant.* Adrian always gunned out the deepest moguls with reckless speed. His knees sprung to his chest like bullets, his boots held tight together and with the biggest, boyish grin washing over his face as he flew the jumps in twisters and spread eagles. He could land solidly, purposefully, with all the confidence of an athlete who knew how to make winning look easy. Propped on his poles at the bottom of the run, he stared up at me, his braces glinting through his smile. *Come on, Shane!* – he called – *Hit it dead centre and you'll fly when you hit the lip!* I envied him then, I remember, envied those braces even, linking his teeth like miniature scaffolds. How he knew he had the talent so couldn't give a fuck about anything else.

Somewhere down the platform, shouts emerge from an administration office. The static of radios crackles the heat as a squadron of officers pushes from the far end through groups of lingering travellers. The brass details on their military insignia flash as they cut through slats of sunlight angled from the ventilation shafts. As they vanish into the room, drafts of pigeons suddenly loose from the rafters and flap across the stone canopy, arching as one body into a frantic grey landing – a chorus of warbles pecking crumbs from the ochre tile. Squatting at the wall, a toothless woman fans a pot of curry she balances on a charcoal tin. She nods at me, opens her cruddy gums and heaves a laugh in my direction, bringing her hands to her sides in the shape of two gnarled wings: She flaps and laughs again.

More shouts as the crowd outside the office grows, each man craning to see inside. Curious, I stand, walk down the platform and join the peering men. On the administrator's desk inside the room sits a small television, its wire antennae kinked and taped to the plaster wall. The screen flickers a newscast of a street scene deep in Pakistan – the grime-caked city of Peshawar. The crowd jostles its heat around me, a human herd damp with beards and turbans, ciphers of Urdu, Pashto and Punjabi. I glance back at my skis left propped against the wall. Strange to see them meet this foreignness, so far from their mountains, so far from where they'd lain for ten years in my garage next to garden hoses, bags of birdseed, rakes and bicycles.

A voice calls out behind me – You are going to Peshawar? You must alter your plans if you are.

When I turn I meet the face of a young man, brown and boyish-skinned. Black hair sweeps across his forehead; he is dressed in an olive-green shalwar with eyes the clear tourmaline of glaciers. His black lashes draw out a hint of moustache.

—I would not go to Peshawar if I were you – he continues – Not today.

—Islamabad, but not until this evening. What happened there?

He pushes in front of a row of grey-bearded men and stands next to me – The Taliban made an assault. A prison has been attacked and they have freed nearly four hundred convicts. I am afraid now Pakistan is very dangerous for you. They will cancel the train to Peshawar until more notice.

—And for Islamabad?

—Wait, wait. I will ask – he presses through to the window. After a jabber of Urdu, the office attendant nods his head, waving him away disinterestedly.

The boy pushes back to me – There is still a train to Islamabad. This evening, yes.

—Good – I extend him my hand – That's good. I'm Shane.

—Sahir. And from Islamabad, where will you go?

—Gilgit and the Karakoram.

—I knew it. The mountains – Sahir's face frees into a smile. Like the son of some Kashmiri diplomat with high Zoroastrian cheekbones, his teeth are starched, untarnished, shockingly aligned. A descendent of handsome, high-nosed Greeks left in his bloodline from Alexander the Great, he stands like a vintage postcard against the backdrop of the station – They are beautiful, that is what I hear.

—It's why I came.

—We in Pakistan are very proud of our country. More so, we are proud of the foreigners who dare to come here.

But you are alone and there are serious dangers for people of your flesh tone. Your skin is more valuable to some than a tiger's.

—Everyone prefers to dress themselves in the hides of other animals. My friend Akram, he's late. He's taking me to Islamabad this evening.

—Then you have time for a tour of Lahore station – Sahir brightens – I'm sure you must be curious about many things in our history. As my father tells me, it is peace for the soul to revisit the cages of our past as different men.

ASR – 2:40 PM

It was nearing the end of first term when the smell of winter hit the air. Something metallic, zinc or nickel, signalled the snow was about to fall. While everyone else dreaded the approaching cold, Adrian and I plotted the length of the coming ski season, how many weekends still ahead, how many runs. We sketched out the tricks we wanted to master in elaborate coloured diagrams. It felt good to embrace what others wouldn't, to love something others rejected.

The bright fluorescents of the hallway stoked the red lockers as Adrian came up to me, pulling me into the empty computer lab.

—Check this out – he grinned in the darkness – Guess who.

His phone's screen had a series of messages from a number I didn't recognize.

—*Looking forward to the season?*

—*Sure. I'm keen to try the 360.*

—*360's for big boys. Got an extra pair of those boxers you wear?*

—*Dozens. Why? They're Costco. U want some?*

—*I meant for the 360. But you offering?*

—*Got some old pairs. Yours if you want them.*

—*My kind of guy. Send a pic in them first if you feel up for it.*

The force of my heart swallowed my eardrums; something sour, thick and unquenchable sucked the moisture off my tongue.

—Mr. Mason?

—Yep.

—Holy shit…

—Got a bunch more like these. Creepy, huh?

—Yeah, for sure. Creepy.

I felt kinked in the thorax, that place where on an insect its thinness is so frightening you fear its body will snap in two. The light from Adrian's phone caught his braces like a diamond mine. I wanted braces more than ever after that, I remember. I caressed the invisible cores of metal I longed to be cemented to my teeth. Calcium, frostbit aluminum, the galvanized steel poles of a schoolyard fence I'd once pressed my tongue to on a dare. The yank of pink flesh, the frostbitten drool of panic, a pale, glacier-hued odour of snow.

—But who cares anyway. He's a perv, so what's the harm, right? – Adrian bit the phone, exposing his teeth – He's pushing me hard this season and I need him to get me ready for Junior's. Turin is in five years. What do you think, can you believe it? Mason is friends with the coach of the Canadian team. You know what it would mean to make the Olympics? I've got a shot at it, you know that, right?

—Don't say anything – I prayed my breath hadn't quickened – Not to anyone.

⟡

Sahir leads me from the departure platform to the main hall teeming with passengers, his hand outstretched behind him – Come, come. I will show you something you cannot see in palaces. This way, Shane.

My skis are hoisted on my shoulder; my duffel bag packed with snow gear hangs from me like a harness. Rivulets of heat breach the back of my shirt. We cross through a series of anterooms stocked with bundles and parcels in knotted fabric, torn-taped, walling in clans of seated women in shalwars of purple, tangerine and emerald, obliterating themselves with jewelled dupatta scarves.

—We still have many problems since partition – Sahir says – When we Muslims left India we gave our hearts to Lahore. Even then, as symbolic as this city is, it too has seen its share of violence – he points at the floor for emphasis – There have been bombs, explosions, here in this station.

—When the Muslims left India?

—Bodies clogged the aisles, under the seats, even filling the lavatories. When the Bombay Express arrived here, no person remained alive except one. One survivor of two thousand – the engineer, an Englishman. The Sikhs from Bhatinda massacred them. Do you know what it means to give your heart to something others want dead?

—You have beautiful areas too – I say – The Himalayas, Biafo, the Karakoram. That's where I'm going to ski.

—There are many mountains here, but not many who are fortunate enough to be skiers. Leave your things in this office. I will show you something special from this swelter- ing cage I am kept in.

Sahir turns down a corridor to a musty room where a turbaned man squats amid stacks of baggage reading a newspaper – He is my friend, don't worry. He will watch your things for no charge while we finish the tour, yes?

Without my bags, the cool of the midday breeze hits the damp of my shirt. I feel the lightness that comes from hav- ing set down the heaviest loads, the freedom of moving for- ward unencumbered.

Outside the rear of the station, we stand on an aban- doned platform of cracked asphalt. Leggy weeds flower in the baking sun; pigeons warble somewhere in the eaves. Steel tracks wander the yard unused like the ruts of forgot- ten wagons. There is a quiet here that feels almost rural. I look out at the yard's fence line, to the clusters of soot-caked buildings and edifices of peeling advertisements for Punjabi action films and soda brands. Hitched to an orange cart, the semitonal haw of a donkey tumbles the fence from a side street. From beneath the haze emerge the spired domes and sunburnt turrets of the Emperor's Mosque, the low wail of the noontime call to prayer. Farther still in the distant hills, those prisoners of Peshawar running free. What trains were pulled along these tracks, I think? What massacred people?

—Come this way – Sahir jumps onto the gravel hugging the rail ties so solid and brimful with history – Quickly, Shane. This way!

To our right, a row of carriages pulls from the station; an engine chugs and draws, heaving its massive weight forward. As it accelerates, a line of men sprints beside it, grabbing onto the handholds, leaping up and inside. One after the other as the train speeds up, the men are pulled up to the roof by the hands of those crouching on top, their shalwars flapping in the breeze.

—We men love to take chances, don't we? – Sahir looks back at me – You must take risks to feel the full rewards of freedom, don't you agree?

He flashes a grin, startling and familiar. Behind him, the train capped with turbaned men disappears into the hot smog of Lahore.

MAGHRIB – 4:59 PM

I remember that feeling of relief when Mr. Mason's texts began arriving to my phone as well. He had the numbers of all the skiers on the team to reach us in case we lost track of time or wandered off-piste, to rein in an energetic flock of boys released across the mountainside. Relief, I remember, galvanized into a kind of pride I could only share with Adrian. I remember walking through the hallways, taller, dragging my hand along the lockers, trying to suppress a grin.

—*Nice practice today. Feeling more confident?*

—*Yeah, felt like I improved my approach a lot.*

—*You're not as brave as the others. You play it safe. It shows in your speed.*

—*I like to know what I'm doing before I try a new trick. Speed's fine, I guess.*

—*Risk isn't for everyone. We'll have to loosen you up next time.*

—*Yeah, I could use that. I tighten up when I'm nervous.*

—*Bet you're tight a lot of places* :)

Something drew down in Adrian's face as he read, the muscles around his lips tightening into the flexes of a scowl.

—You ever send him that picture? – I asked – I'm thinking I should send him one too.

—It's true – Adrian stepped back, suddenly bolder – You don't take enough chances. That's what makes you such a lousy skier anyways. If it were up to you, you'd just follow in my tracks the whole way down.

—What? No way.

—You can't even do a simple spread eagle. And the whole team has to baby you on a twist.

—Fine, I won't take one. Who even cares?

That night at practice the snow was ice crystals and pellets; they shot through the air like artillery, soaked our jackets and formed a stubborn drag our skis resisted. I didn't ride the lift with Adrian. I watched him a few chairs ahead scraping at the slush on his ski with his pole, the slope's lights dim aureoles behind the blizzard. Later, I looked down to see Mr. Mason coaching Adrian at the kicker. I felt sick, snapped in two, when Adrian launched into the air, spun and landed a 360. I watched Mr. Mason ski down and shake him by his shoulders, cheering. The snow's wetness permeated my gloves, my jacket, my hoodie, my T-shirt to my skin, the chairlift carrying me deeper into the clouds.

Two weeks later, Adrian found me by my locker. His eyes were red with the remnants of tears he'd wiped away quickly, his posture a strange blend of the macho I admired him for and the skulking of a scraped-kneed boy.

—I'm off the team – his lashes were damp clumps – Fuck those motherfuckers. Suspended too.

—What do you mean? Who?

—Mr. Mason and Mr. Lucas. I just had a meeting in the principal's office. All three called me in. Cocksuckers kicked me off the team.

—What? What for?

—It was just an old roach, not even a joint. Mr. Lucas caught me behind the portable yesterday. He took me to the office right away, stoned as hell – he rubbed his thumb along the metal edge of my open locker – You've got to help me, Shane. I'm a dick for saying you were a shit skier, but you've got to help me. I'm not giving up Turin for one lousy roach – he sniffed; it sounded like he loaded a rifle – Did you save those messages? The ones from Mr. Mason?

I remember the hallway turning dark and tubular, red as guts, the doorway at the end a far and unreachable galaxy. In my ears I heard the ski lift ratcheting us up to a peak we'd never skied or ever dared to.

It was the right thing to do, to help Adrian, I persuaded myself, though for nights I didn't sleep or slept fitfully, waking in tangled intervals embroidered with craving and dread. Success begs to be shared, I reasoned, so we should abandon our fear, we should face the enemy. Square and emboldened, I grew to want Turin for Adrian as much as he did. I fortified his plan because I feared losing him from the team, feared holding a secret I couldn't share with anyone if he left. We agreed to show the messages to our parents, to allow them to contact school authorities, to confront Mr. Mason together.

Still, in memory, those days are a collection of images edited together like old camcorder video. The way my mother's fork touched her plate as it trembled, how she left the pots in the sink and went to bed early. How in the meeting Mr. Mason was stone-faced and I searched him for fissures of anger, betrayal, hurt, but found none. Pillared between our parents, we shielded our phones in our palms, charged and sweaty with evidence. How Adrian was asked to load his photographs onto a laptop, to stand squinting beneath the alien light of the projector as it cast a pale image of his bony torso in boxer shorts onto the chalkboard. How I was asked to stand and do the same for the images on mine. Both of us were silent, teary-eyed travellers in confrontation with a part of the world we'd dropped ourselves into yet couldn't comprehend, a planet abuzz with such strangeness it paralyzed us to the bone. How the principal's voice crumbled the air at last saying, *That's fine now, boys. That will do.* How the clock above us froze in the fluorescents, how the texture of shame knotted the carpets, the chalk dust, the sound of handcuffs clicking shut. How neither of us could lift ourselves to look as the policemen led Mr. Mason from the room. How the red rotation of the cruiser's lights flashed off the classroom's unfamiliar surfaces. How the guilt of a consequence could be so much worse than the crime.

Adrian and I were asked to be present for the arraignment hearing. The list of charges looped in my head like the coaching mantras I replayed before a downhill run: *Luring and invitation to sexual touching involving minors. Commission and possession of child pornography.*

—You sent him those kinds of photos? – I whispered.

Adrian toyed with the end of his tie – Who cares?

A strange expression played around his face and it took me a moment to notice. He looked over at me and smiled without smiling, running his tongue across his teeth, newly smooth, porcelain-straight.

—Holy shit – I whispered.

Mr. Mason pled not guilty and posted his bail.

ISHA – 6:25 PM

—The most special thing about Pakistan is that we men are free to do as we please – Sahir lights a cigarette and kicks an empty bottle through the stalky weeds in the gravel – Do you smoke?

—No, thank you.

—We rule the land as birds over a valley. We are free to jump onto the tracks, to chase whatever train we wish to catch. Do you see what I mean?

—That's why I ski, to find a piece of that feeling – I answer. A feeling like I've left the earth for a moment, flown, gained a softer perspective of snow and ice and blazing altitude, to subdue something powerful, force it into forgiving me.

—I have always wished to ski – Sahir says – Yet that is dangerous too. A few days ago in Kashmir an avalanche swallowed nearly two hundred soldiers. They ski down the glaciers from post to post with their rifles, the highest military base in the world. Do you believe that? Guarding the mountains as if someone would steal them.

—Dangerous – I say – There is nowhere safe in the universe.

With his cigarette Sahir gestures out at the reddish haze above the city, the vibrations of the muezzin's calls crippling the dusk – May I ask why you came here? Why Pakistan?

Clouds of crystalline powder shower the slope as the metal edges of our skis shave the alpine skin to blue flesh. Utter wilderness and exhilaration, to explore the exploded heartbeat instead of fleeing from it. To find freedom from gravity, from consequences. Although a decade ago, I want Adrian to know that when the news came on, Mr. Mason's face was a cyan-magenta-yellow rendering above the text: ACCUSED TEACHER KILLED BY TRAIN, LAYS HIMSELF ON TRACKS DAYS BEFORE TRIAL. That I cried for us all as I read and vomited until I was hoarse. That I lay at the toilet's pedestal, heaving and exhausted, that I ran my astringent tongue across my teeth and thought of him. That I nurtured no resentment, no envy, when years later I heard he'd made the team for Turin. That I wheeled a friend's television seven blocks in a shopping cart to the house where I boarded in college to watch his qualifying round. That I gasped when I saw his skis contact ice and his legs fly out from under him and his body flail above the rippled braid of mounded snow, an impossible matrix of limbs and poles and catastrophe. That I felt it all for him as if it had been me.

—Have you ever heard of ghosts? They're thin and white and made of air. They follow you to the ends of the earth crying out for things you can't give. I thought they couldn't follow me here but they did.

—They will only leave you in peace once you submit – the blue of Sahir's eyes is clear as an iceberg – Yes, ghosts. We in Pakistan know them well but it is in both of our interests that we learn to coexist. We must strive to become better men, no matter the cage of our past. What is wrong? You look as though your mule has run. Are you sad for something?

—No – I say – Just done, just through with phantoms. Tired and anxious. I want to ski.

—Your train too – Sahir says, standing – We must begin looking for your friend.

The departure hall seems aged ten years. Families sprawl asleep amid the baggage; swarms of insects tick against the ceiling fans, their husks piling the corners of the floor in drifts. Re-entering the station, I breathe in that same feeling I had when stranded at school late at night after practice. Something dark and empty coated the familiar corridors yet made them seem kinder, less school somehow, more sanctuary. I try to picture Sahir's boyhood days, the classrooms he studied and recited in, the moths that flicked along the sills as he chanted the Koran or memorized the dates of old massacres, the ghosts of his country stalking the land beyond the window.

—You see, your things are safe – Sahir leads me into the baggage room. My skis and duffel bag are propped in the corner, dim relics in a museum archive – If you like, I will carry them for you. Don't worry, I don't ask that you pay me, this is my pleasure.

Sahir runs his hands over the lacquered finish of the planks, reading the binding mechanism, thumbing the edges' razor.

—And in here? – he weighs the duffel.

—The boots. They're heavy. I'll take them.

He ignores me, hooking the straps over one shoulder. He tucks the skis beneath his arm, his grin the widest Cheshire – It really is my pleasure.

When we approach the main hall, Akram is propped against the wall staring at the platform congested with pigeons. Small and agile, he looks like a bespectacled tour guide in charge of an unruly gaggle of kids. He exhales when he sees me, comes to his feet and opens his arms for a hug.

—Oh, my God, Shane. Can you believe this country? – his arms pull tight around me – We're supposed to be glad the British left but I can't see a single redeeming benefit if the trains don't run on time.

—It's good you're here. I spent the day with Sahir.

Sahir stands at my side holding the skis, the duffel bag, looking on as though trying to decipher a code.

—*Assalaamu alaykum* – Akram gestures to him – But it's not fine, Shane. My train was supposed to arrive eight hours ago. You've been waiting all day and I'm afraid it's all for nothing. We can't even go to Islamabad.

—What? What for?

—The expedition's been cancelled. That bloody prison break, didn't you hear? The Taliban has freed the lot of them, terrorists and kidnappers, isn't that right? The Consulate wants us out. Too dangerous, they say. Well how bloody dangerous is a glacier anyway? You won't find Al-Qaeda on skis, will you? I'm sorry you came all this way, but it's finished. Awful, I know.

—Finished? That's it?

—Adrian's fuming. You can't imagine how livid he is. The poor man is convinced he'll never get to ski another day in his life. I don't blame him. But thank God you came when you did. This train is the Samjhauta leaving for Attari. We'll be back to civilization in under an hour if we catch it. Shane. What a hellhole. We'd have been better off in Nepal despite the Maoists. Come, I've already bought you a ticket.

The departure hall reverberates with the announcer's voice amplified off the heat and stone. Carriages creak and snap at their hitches, their wheels popping free of inertia as the train begins to roll.

—Come on, Shane. It would crush me to have to spend the night here.

Sahir jogs with me beside the doors of the moving carriage, the skis and duffel bag large and unwieldy.

—You jump inside – he says – I will pass them to you. Go now. You see it's speeding up.

Running with the carriage, the train accelerates as Akram leaps aboard. I grab hold of the bar beside the door, jump and pull myself up and inside.

—Your skis first… – Sahir shouts, running.

—Keep them – I say – They're yours.

The steady clack of rails, its rocking speed, the sudden end of the asphalt platform like a precipice leapt and flown from. Sahir comes to a standstill, his green shalwar looped in the straps of my bags as we pull away into the cinder-bricked suburbs of Lahore graffitied by curls of Urdu script. Back to India, I think, to the safety of borders.

—You're as good as a pro – Akram says as we catch our breaths – Few Indians will even play at that game, and even then only the crazy ones. But Shane, why did you give him those skis? That boy won't be able to use them in a thousand years.

—To give him something to flee with – I think – To save himself, to outrun avalanches.

—Thank God we didn't have to spend the night. A bloody hellhole, I tell you.

A train rumbles and sways in the kind of cadence the body remembers. In the seats ahead, the saris of women ripple in the evening breeze. Akram's head tilts to his chest in a doze. Already I feel the new growth of stubble roughen my chin, the border of India fifty kilometres ahead in the dusk, the passing farmland statued with goats and waddles of geese being led to their grassy creeks by shepherds in white turbans.

I wake in the night as the train suddenly slows. We crawl forward in approach to a crowd, a hundred men, semi-circular, crammed tight to the tracks. The sea of their faces passes my window near enough I smell the heat off their skin. In the mass of them, I swear I see one with the face of Mr. Mason, cold-eyed, acquitting, the whites of his irises flashing at me beneath police lights. There is the flapping of furious wings against my stomach, a whole flock panicking as one bird falls in a spray of feathers, hooked by the predator's claws. Through a break in the crowd, there is a dune of cloth and severed flesh, the dusty heap of a man on the tracks, his shalwar soaked in red, the skin of his feet, still in sandals, turned grey.

Erin Soros

MORNING
IS VERTICAL

Desolation Sound

There is no horizon in the woods. Morning is vertical.
The sun does not rise or set but is a jagged flicker between
trees. It shoots through cedars and firs two hundred feet tall,
wide branches shattering the light until it smashes on the
forest floor.

Night. Day. Yellow specks, the ground still dark between them.

If a man saw the dawn he could say it was spraying like
a waterfall, he could say the branches cut teeth into it like
the sharp edge of a Swedish fiddle, he could say it opens like
a woman's fan, a narrow tip, the light rippling wide. Sun
spends itself and still it cannot flood the green. Sword ferns
curl in shadow. The trees are five hundred years old. The
trees are one thousand years old. The trees are thick dark
columns that remain dark. And time too is vertical, not
rolling slowly forward on a path but branching up, rooting
down. Black fat beetles tunnel eyeless under damp rocks
and the flies wake, their blue-bottle eyes prehistoric.

Sitka spruce, western hemlock, western red cedar,
Douglas fir – *Doug fir* we call it as if the tree were not large

enough to kill us in its fall. Now dark moss hangs thick from its branches in great sheets that turn the air blue-green. Now pale moss hangs spindly and thin and fades to white. We call it Old Man's Beard, and we tug it off the bark and throw it over our heads and stomp through the forest veiling it behind us.

But the trees are not men; the trees are the trees and their trunks will grow for another five hundred years, one thousand years, each tree swelling wide enough to hold a coffin and shrink any man's death.

There is Tin Hat Mountain. It is not yet old. Unnecessary Mountain is not yet old. There is time buckling in the coastal forest, land butting up from the ocean long ago when sea plates crashed the shore, centuries unburied into this one. Rock meets rock and lifts, the way water forms waves under pressure. The mountains are fierce rough carvings, uneven and unfinished; these are not the volcanic spheres of Mount Ranier or Mount Shasta, their angelic symmetry peeking through clouds; these are not the soft scrubbed hills of Eastern Canada that a man can walk right over; these coastal mountains are ancient oceans folding up ten thousand feet to scrape the sky, peaks born anew in the haphazard violence of the West.

Before us came the glaciers cutting fresh scars into rock then retreating without softening these hills that are too steep to let anything rest. Long before us this old land had been folded and scraped new by the land's own force and now it attracts new men, immigrants from Iceland and Sweden and Norway, from Hungary and Wales, all of us from the Old World arriving as rough and unfinished as the land we've come to shape.

We came in waves as the glaciers came in waves, sweeping over this forest to tear it down.

British Columbia. There was nothing British about it.

We felled the spruce and the fir and the cedar and still we could not see the sun. We built a paper mill; we built a dam; we built a surge tank.

The surge tank is three hundred feet high, holding water to release pressure from the dam, a rush of water tumbling in a funnel down the mountain until it reaches the tank where it cannot join the ocean, cannot reach that final vast release, and so the speed of the water can force it only up, up.

There is Suicide Cliff. There is Desolation Sound. We are not in the flat wide middle of this country; we are pressed to its edge.

Crummy

The crummy is a flatbed truck, open-backed, with sides built from slats of cedar, a roof of corrugated steel. As the truck balances around the steep curves of the mountain road on a morning like this – dark, another hour yet before sunlight – it rumbles hollow although we are packed man-to-man inside. We sit on four cedar benches, one bench against each side and two together running down the middle, ten loggers to a bench – the lucky ones leaning against the shaking walls, the unlucky sitting in the middle, back to back, nodding off to snooze with only another man's spine for support. The worst spot is next to the open end of the crummy where the air swirls with dust and exhaust. The seat next to the driver is prime territory, especially in winter, but even in summer it is prized for its leather cushion and its windows that keep out the weather and the dust. That seat is reserved for the high rigger, sometimes a hooker or a faller, never one of the chokers, chasers or buckers or any of the young men who do not have the skill of the old ones. They know their place is here in the rear of the truck.

This week we did not need the hazard stick to tell us we would be on early shift. We could feel it in the dryness of the air, static crackle of pine cones underfoot, that faded summer smell of woods like paper waiting to flame. Hazard is high. The high rigger announced the change yesterday while we stood trackside waiting for the crummy to bring us down. We would need to be back up the hill by four the next morning so we could finish our shift before the day's full heat turned the woods into kindling. This is government policy, not that of the camp, and we all suspect that the Mac-Blo company would just as soon keep us working on the mountain till we burned.

Last night the cook made roast beef and we ate enough to weight us to our chairs. We played poker and smoked and listened to Jack Benny and tried to squeeze as much time out of the evening as we could. Then we were up at three, in the crummy as soon as we'd had our fill. We will arrive trackside when dawn waits at the edge of the woods and then we will have to hike for another forty minutes in the glimmering light – fallers and buckers hefting their axes and saws while the chokers and hookers carry the choker cables and choker bells that are needed to replace the ones that broke – and by five we will reach the cold-deck pile where the logs are stacked and our paid work can begin.

But now we are invisible in the dark. No one is tracking our time. There is nothing yet to cut or choke and we can lean against another man's back and nod into whatever shallow sleep the bouncing truck will allow. We will have to be up at three again tomorrow and the morning after that, eating stacks of flapjacks when we are too tired to chew. Then we sit in this crummy in a waking sleep that rocks with the rocking of the truck until it seems that night is not a time but a place we inhabit and that daylight lies so far from our bunks that we must all be woken and fed and trucked these dim hours up the mountain if we are ever to see the sun.

One man has a headache, another man's spine is rattled sore with each bump of the road, and the shaking of the crummy makes us all clench our teeth while the stinking exhaust gets sucked into the back of the truck, but we know that the morning beyond the crummy is grey-blue and sharp, not smoke-filled and angry with the summer's orange flames, and we are glad to be travelling to work not with hoses and buckets for water but with axes and saws. The space between the benches is so narrow that our knees tap against each other and we catch another man's eye and nod that the day has begun.

This morning we ride with the new hook tender. He is here to replace Charlie, our own sly Charlie Chaplin – the only one among us who named himself. His replacement sits in the middle of the truck straight as a tent pole. He arrives on early shift when the mountain is dressed for mourning, the sky dark as we sneak the new man past the trees. Forty men sit around him as if we could offer him the protection we failed to give the last one.

We all recall the wind and the rain of the day that took Charlie, and we all know there are times when we do not need a hazard stick to tell us that danger is near, just as there are mornings when a man wakes and feels dread not of today or tomorrow but of a day that is already gone and he waits for what the light will bring that he cannot quite remember, but he knows, even in his sleep he knows, that he has done something wrong and he fears that the morning will let him see it. Any man has had dreams when he wants to run but his legs and arms cannot move and he wants to scream but his lips will not open and he wakes trembling with the failure of his will.

We read the hazard stick for the future, not the past. In the woods a day is new and death is erased like the chalk dust that billows up from the road and falls as soon as the crummy has passed. Charlie's replacement doesn't know this camp and its stories. His mind isn't chipped like the crummy's wooden floor worn into sawdust by the spikes of our boots.

An apple falls from someone's tin pail. We watch it bounce out the back of the truck. The crummy grinds up the last one hundred yards that pitch steep and unforgiving. Dust from the road swirls inside the crummy to cover us the colour of chalk so when we finally reach trackside and the engine stops – there it is, that sliver of a sun, the welcoming chatter of birds – we crawl stiff from the crummy into the morning's grey-blue light and we shake off this white dust like men carved new from stone.

Tin Men

In summer we call her the ice cream ship. She's the same vessel that comes up coast all the other seasons, a plume of steam dragging through the sky every two weeks bringing food, kerosene, men. From May Day to Labour Day she carries ice cream. Proper, store-bought, Vancouver ice cream. The furnace room walls are sweating, but on the second level the freezers are lined with vanilla as smooth and white as the hull.

The high rigger is the first to see her. Strapped to the peak of the spar tree he's just topped, its tip crashing to the ground like the face of a mountain, he wipes the glare from his eyes to peer out across the ocean and there she is.

Summer. Saturday. Cedar branches spread motionless in the stagnant air. "Coming in," the high rigger shouts, his hands a funnel around his mouth. "She's coming in!" The chaser and the chokers turn toward the sea.

From where the hooking crew stands, they see nothing but trees. Not the high rigger half a mile away, not the faller and bucker working uphill. The high rigger's voice crests then dips, amplified by the mountain that arches behind him. Unhooking his rope he sits on the spar's tip, a cylinder ten inches wide and two hundred feet high, his boots crossed at the ankle.

It's another hour before the ship nudges into the bay. Distances are deceptive in the woods. We have time to ride the crummy to the camp and then shave, smoke, before we catch the railway speeder the last six miles down. We are Camp B, up Tin Hat Mountain. The loggers from the other camp are already standing restless by the water. We jump off the speeder where the rail line meets the shore. Without spikes our town boots feel new and slick on sand. We wear canvas pants, leather suspenders, clean cotton shirts. The Swedes and Norwegians are tanned bark-brown and the Scots are sunburned. We nod at the other loggers. We watch the ship dock.

The ship lowers a long metal limb. It stirs the air so that a hundred feet away the warm stench hits us. Rancid meat, although we know the smell isn't meat, and isn't coming from the ship. The air is thick with it. The greenhorns gag, tongues pressed to the roof of their mouths. We all cover our noses with fists or palms.

"Is it always this bad?"

The coffins are made of tin, and the sun reflects off each sharp angle.

"Jesus, they'll be fried in there like strips of bacon."

Two weeks the coffins have waited. They line the dock now in a tidy row: a high rigger, a faller, and four of a fire crew. The West Coast – White Rock to the panhandle – takes two loggers a day. The inlets of the province are studded with tin men.

Last night a group of boys dared each other to run up and down the dock, and to prove they'd done it they plunked rocks and driftwood on top of each tin box, as if the bodies were not heavy enough to weigh the coffins down.

None of us can see the names. We know the loggers in the tins, though not by what their mothers call them. We know the smell of their skin in the bunkhouse, who butters both sides of his bread and who gets quiet in thunder. Almost all the men are rechristened the moment they set foot in the camp. Step-and-a-half because he limps. Tangoola because he has long monkey arms and the name sounds like the jungle. Seaball, no one knows why. Snowball, so Seaball would have a twin. One-eyed-Pete, who had one eye, we sometimes called One – *Hey One, hand me the Swede.* When a logger dies, the clerk announces his real name, both the front and the back – *Who has Rolf Jensen's boots now? He hasn't paid out.* His birth name is naked, how the clerk says it too loud.

The winch angles back and forth from ship to wharf like a steel elbow. A wooden box splits open, the cans spilling out and nudging against the coffins, as if the tin were magnetic, metal finding metal. Children from the mill town cheer as sailors roll the frozen tubs down the length of the wharf, the sailors' hands sticking to the frost. They run to meet the ice cream, then slow and back away when they meet that smell. A girl begins to cry.

The younger men always eat too fast, and the pain shoots through their sinuses. The first bite of ice cream – a double cone for each logger – and they can feel it in the back of their eyes.

Erin Soros

The winch loads the coffins. The first one twirls slightly, hanging uneven, the head heavier than the feet. As each coffin is lifted, the driftwood and rocks on the lids fall and splash.

Boys stand knee-deep in the ocean, one spitting a mouthful of ice cream to see if it will float. The sailors drag the containers away from the wharf so the women are clear of the smell. Ice-vapor rises in front of their dresses as they scoop deeper. We hide our stumped fingers, missing thumbs, behind the cones, so the ladies won't see.

Blackie has all his fingers. Cat's Paw lost four, but he still works the steam donkey. The thumb is the worst. Without one it is hard even to hold a cone. Any man would trade three fingers for a thumb.

In this way we know each other. How a hand holds an ice cream, how a nickname recalls a scar. If a man is injured on a hill, there'd be a couple loggers allowed to carry him down, but if a man dies, we drag the body to the cold-deck pile and keep falling the trees. Company policy. No point wasting the day. The logger stiffens and grows cold. Sometimes a branch falls across the body, and we are careful to lever it off.

At dinner in the cookhouse after a day like that, we are quiet. His sweat dries in his undershirt draped across the bunkhouse window. The curve of his spine dips the cot.

Two weeks later we meet the ice cream ship and pass his nickname to a new logger. *Hey, One-Eyed*, we call to a man who has two.

Fall

The first drop of rain is quiet, tentative, falling like a question a man could convince himself he has not heard.

Autumn hovers. The sky rests heavy above us though we still walk on pine needles dry from the day's heat.

Rain on the donkey's metal skin.

Then rain darkens leather and swells our flannel pockets. Our wet wool socks blister our heels. Rain falls in eyes, on lips, on shoulders, in creeks down our backs now wet in that tender spot on the upper spine shivering a man's hands that grip a saw beaded with rain.

Each time the faller hacks his ax into the back cut, his face is sprayed with water that spits from the gouge. When the back cut is open, two fallers jam a piece of wood into it to direct the tree's lean. Then they start with a new cut on the reverse. They drop their axes and pick up a two-handled saw, one man on either end of the grey horizontal line. Their sawing shakes the branches so water dumps onto their hats and shoulders. Bark is slick. The moss that grows on the bark is sodden. The fallers balance on slippery springboards on either side of the trunk and they pull the misery whip back and forth, back and forth, its teeth stubborn against the wet wood. The spray of water paces each pull.

The tree splashes when it hits the ground.

Soon the rain will pockmark the roads and float pine needles to the sea. Soon water will bloat the earth, this soft crumbling shell of wet dirt lying between us and the sea that threatens to open under our boots.

Through the fall and winter and spring, it will rain. Twenty days in a row, forty days in a row, rain so constant that the air itself is rain. We wring our undershirts, leaving puddles on the bunkhouse floor that steam in the stove's heat. Outside, fungus roots the trees. Inside, even our skin grows its own strange mould, darkening in brown patches on our chests, backs, armpits, groins, wherever the skin is welcoming and moist.

Daylight is too tired to rise. The sun sleeps its day under clouds grey as the dank blankets that tangle our cots. We rise. We work in rain with our pants hanging heavy at the knee. Our canvas shirts stiffen wet into tortoise shells. Any light that manages to struggle through the trees is lit green by branches the way light in the ocean shines green.

The summer's trees lie scattered on the ground – felled, bucked, waiting to be choked. We work where solid earth ends at the coast, where mist rises and rain falls until a man could believe there is no division between land and water, that even this last wet line on the map is gone.

Roll of Bills

On the morning of Christmas Eve, the logging camp shuts down. The generator dies – quiet splits the year – and we are on the *Queen Mary* with our cards, with the booze we've smuggled on the ship, another brown-paper purchase each time the motors slow and we run down the platform through the stink of oil and into a beer parlour and then back inside.

Drink up, it's Christmas! Drink up, we've escaped!

The camp is back in the woods, dim as a cataract. The bunkhouses, the wooden sidewalks, the cookhouse, the commissary, all quiet and dark and empty of men. There will be no falling for a week. No bucking, no donkey loading, no rigging. Seven days we are free. We sit inside the ship's smoky warmth and don't watch the mountains that pass us by. We toast the holiday with our bottles of whiskey and flick our cards and come to fisticuffs with all the pent-up energy of no work as the engines hum us to the city.

Our celebration has no need for a Christmas tree – who'd want the smell of pine if you're not being paid to cut it down? On the ship we review what we've bought and what we are going to buy – whiskey, rum, a cozy twelve-pack of beer to furnish our hotel room. A man needs something to wake up for in the morning. Those who don't talk about the booze are already drinking serious and can hardly let their lips off their bottlenecks to toast the day.

Vancouver. Port town, party town. Open up and let us in.

Through the ship's rain-streaked glass we see the red neon "W" twirling two hundred feet above the sea. "Woodward's" is another name for money, a twelve-storey building with windows row on row. But in the dark just this single letter shines to greet us: red legs stretched wide.

We're off the ship and on streets that cannot absorb the rain. It slides down brick buildings, down glass buildings higher than a Doug fir. We are used to ground that gives with moisture, water softening dirt until it welcomes our boots. We are used to branches that dump water on us as we pass, and the sound of wood as the saw chews its fibres. But not this slickness, hardness, the harsh rasp of metal as the street-car squeals the shining corners, a noise so cold and hollow it sounds like the rain's own cry.

Then the yeasty smell of donuts steaming circles from the machine.

A crowd of black umbrellas walks toward us. The streets are cramped with high buildings pressing back the fog, the bustle of long-coated men and tight-waisted women – the men turtling their necks into their collars to keep out the wet, the ladies red-cheeked from their hours in the shops, gripping cranky children as they crush with a gust of warm air through the swinging doors. Everyone buying for some-one.

A small boy bends over to pry at a wad of gum flattened into the sidewalk. His mother swats him, packages spilling out of her bag.

Beneath the lights and noise and the rainbows on the oil slicking water that eddies at the curb, there is the blank screen of this city. Merry Christmas! Merry Christmas! Walk on these streets too long and a man feels the pavement through his spine.

We scatter. To the beer parlours and the dance clubs, through Jap Town and Chinatown, past the neon signs for the Ovaltine Café and the White Lunch, past the neon sign – the giant happy glowing pig – for Save-On-Meats, its carcasses hanging like red curtains in the glass, and on to the Harlem Nocturne and the Smiling Buddha, the streets shimmering and tipping in the rain.

Then we get a look at the ladies. Soft white narrow creatures, women sipping their drinks and slow-rocking their hips. Wall-to-wall mirrors make more and more women, make more of the curves of their bodies than even our eyes can caress. They stand on one side of the bar, men on the other. Crinkle of a cigarette package. Whine of a horn. The air in between the men and women is crackling with Players and brass.

We haven't been this close in months.

Through the smoke they glance at our plaid Macs and dirty fingernails, our jackets pregnant with bottles near on empty. Glenn Miller blares loud enough to lift our heavy boots. It's a pleasure just to watch a lady dab her lipstick and try not to sway, looking over her shoulder and then touching her shoulder as if to give a man permission to do the same.

We are numb and happy. Full of that soft-legged, heavy-tongued ease, we elbow the shy boys toward the prettiest ladies and then saunter outdoors to spit on streets where no spitting is allowed.

Tangoola chicken-walks down Hastings as he tries to find his way to another drink.

Frog raises his bottle to Charlie – *We miss your fiddle on the boat, here's to what tunes you play up there* – then he sells a case of beer to the Indians who lean against the door that says No Indians or Dogs.

Smokey guides his woman up the stairs inside the Patricia, hoping she doesn't catch sight of the crushed mouse on the hallway floor.

And Shakespeare has been rolled, but he doesn't know it yet.

Alone we are uncertain, as watery as the sea's reflection of the Woodward's neon "W."

Christmas Eve means Jester will find himself a whore to offer a ring, just as he did last year and the year before that.

Tell me, love, he asks, *what do they call you at home?*

Christmas morning finds us on cots in the Patricia, without the women we've paid, with the bright glare of sun piercing through curtains thinner than cheesecloth. The city has been cleaned by the rain, but we are not clean, and there returns whatever we tried to drink away. Scratch at the bites around ankles. Rattle the twelve-pack of beer by the bed.

Drink makes wishes roll in our minds like the night rain that covers the buildings, each drop full of sheen from the lights, all that colour that is not the water's own. Hastings, Granville, Seymour, Burrard – the streets of this city are never named for the men who built it. A man could walk these streets and never know of Desolation Sound or Suicide Cliff, could sleep in these buildings and never touch the trees that support the walls. Through the window of Oscar's are signed photographs of Greta Garbo and Rita Hayworth, their lipstick faces alone in empty booths. A few more days through our wads of cash and we're stealing lemon extract. Then we line our debts under the sign for the Logger's Employment Agency, cursing and tipping our hats to its red neon light.

Seagull turd mottles the ship's plank. We kick at it and watch the town folk who do not watch us. They hold their packages and stare right ahead until it seems they are walking with their eyes and not their legs. The turd sticks to our boots like splotches of paint that someone hasn't bothered to spread. The turd stinks. First day of the year, the days not yet filled in.

Some of us sold our boots for booze and so when we board the ship we step up the plank in new boots, fresh laces that tie us in hock to the company store. New Year, new debt. Some of us won't live to make the trip next year, cheating Mac-Blo out of what we owe from our last drunk.

Logging Camp B

We carve our addresses on the slabs of wood that travel to London where soldiers and civilians stand shivering underground, inhaling the armpit closeness of their neighbours and waiting for the long slow whistle of the next bomb. They look up at the cedar walls of their shelters and there we are.

A woman's fingers reach up to rub the words we have carved, the wood splintering her skin just as it so often splinters ours.

The Londoners read the shelter walls and all around them the buildings collapse. In the cramped stinking air they write letters to Camp B as if they could tell their secrets to the alphabet itself. Sometimes their letters smell of talc, sometimes of smoke. An old man writes of his wife and how he misses the way her upper arms shook when she thumped the rolling pin back and forth across the dough. One boy wants us to send him a saw; another tells us his sister isn't a virgin. In the middle of a bombing raid, a woman aborted her child with the end of a broom handle and she writes this nameless fact in black spotty ink and sends it to Stillwater.

Each Sunday we read these letters, the edges darkened by the dirt from our hands, and then we step outside in the cool evening light cast by the camp generator. The air is sweet with pine. We play tug-rope, four men on one side of the knot, four men on the other. The coils twist painfully against our palms and we dig our boots into mud that offers no traction as we feel the rope slip.

Spring

Where the trees were, the white wake-robin is already blooming – scattered bits of paper. A bear paws the dirt, clumsy with sleep. Our smell is on the wind.

In this quarter, new logs lie on the ground, waiting to be bucked, choked, hooked to the cold-deck pile. We've left one tree standing – the highest and straightest – the spar tree, for the high rigger. He works alone. It's a Doug fir, two hundred feet high, as tall as Woodward's neon sign that guards Vancouver's inlet, and our afternoon's entertainment will be to lean back our heads and watch him walk the trunk to the top.

We call him Thorvald, which is really his name. To call him a nickname would be sloppy. He'd just shrug off our attempts.

Today he swats a lazy hand toward our voices, his eyes only for the tree. Barrel-chested and thick-limbed, he's built like a trunk himself. He examines the roots, runs his palm over bark that is creviced deep enough to take his hand. He pulls at the bark, sniffs it, walks the tree's perimeter eyeing each crevice for the stains that warn of cat's face. At this point he could still walk away. A tree can appear healthy on the outside, the bark thick, branches green, and on the inside the cat's face has been rotting the wood through winter and summer, through season after season until the rings at the core disappear into moist crumbling fungus. No man wants to tie himself to a dying tree.

We can tell when Thorvald has made up his mind because he reaches up to press his hat tighter to his head. Then he wraps the high-rigging belt around the trunk and around his hips. He grips the belt, leans back to test its give. He steps forward to jab the spikes of his caulk boots into the bark, shifts his footing, feet splayed, breathing easy just to sense the solid base of the tree under his boots. In these adjustments there is a stillness – he might tweak the belt or check his ax or nod as if to confirm his decision but for a moment it seems his legs are fixed to the tree, that he is growing out of the tree, and would be no more capable of walking away.

He runs. Not away from the tree but straight up the trunk, held by the belt he shares with it, bark spitting a trail beneath him. On the way up he axes off the branches so the tree narrows as he climbs fast as a zipper. We crane our necks, press our hats snug, rocking on solid ground. Some of us reach for chewing tobacco, our cheeks crammed tight, mouths slack in the same awed boredom of circus crowds who grow used to watching men climb into air.

When he reaches the top, he trades his ax for his saw and begins to work away at the fir's wavering tip. It snaps from the trunk. It is twice the length of a man. As it falls, the trunk kicks back. This is the most dangerous part, more deadly than the climb. He's strapped to the tree while it sways back and forth twenty feet to draw a giant arc across the sky. If the core is cracked or weak or rotting, the force will cause the trunk to split in two, and he'll be crushed, boneless, into the tree. We know that high riggers fear this death more than they fear falling.

Today it takes a good ten minutes before the tree stills to vertical. When it does, the clouds keep moving behind it.

Now we can take out a roll-your-own or just roll back our shoulders and stretch. Above us, Thorvald slips off the belt. Easy as a man on a kitchen stool he sits on top of the tree, feet tucked behind him or crossed in front of him, his body tied to nothing. He's having a smoke, or perhaps a sandwich, his satchel in his lap. It's hard to see him from the ground.

Only when he starts waving his hat do we realize he's not sitting but standing – a two-hundred-foot salute – and we know it's this gesture that enables Thorvald to be so quiet in the rest of his day.

We wait for what he does next. The *maypole*, we call this trick: no other man comes down the way he does.

He doesn't come straight down. Belted to the tree and dropping, his boots bouncing off the trunk, he twirls. He corkscrews around and around the tree as he descends, around and around, the bark spraying behind him, his feet wrapping a ribbon around a day's work.

We keep quiet. All we hear is the sound of his boots.

His body appears, then is behind the tree, then appears again, flickers like a zoetrope, the air around him a spiral of bark, his arms gripping the belt and then his hat is floating off and coming down more slowly than he is – he makes one last leap to reach the ground, lands with a grunt, looks up to check the sky, takes a few steps, then holds up his hand to catch the hat.

He lets his high-rigger's belt drop to the ground and jumps out of it two-footed, the way children hop from chalk circles. Then he walks slowly back to us.

Gregory Betts

PLANCK

It's easy to imagine yourself with a superpower, isn't it? You can slip into these fantasies without much convincing, have probably already mapped out the advantages and consequences of various alternatives. But I know how you abandon them when you realize the first genie's twist: super strength leaves you mortal and hungry, seduction prevents you from ever trusting a lover. Jumping, climbing, swimming, even flying, you quickly realize, are just bestial projections. Sun, ice, fire and storms are only elemental. These are the last vestiges of the Greek gods and we have all moved past their moment. Only eventually do you come to realize the advantage shared by all of the comic-book figures, which is their timelessness. This is the real power that pulls us into their mysterious lives, abstract even from their backstories or superficial foibles. Every action of theirs accumulates a history without the cost of history or the consequence. They act and act and act and never scar or age. But imagine tapping into that power, that mystery. Imagine possessing the power to stop time and to move outside of its movement. Not time travel, not local freezes. Time itself unhinged from its ceaseless progression, ever ever more.

Now, imagine that you also give yourself the ability to move freely in this freed moment of time, the freedom of space. It is more complicated than it might at first appear, for what is the moment upon which time might stop? It can be of no duration – therefore it cannot stop upon a second, for a second is a span built of an infinite fan of moments however brief, arrayed in sequential order. You have to push deeper into the splicing of time – down through milliseconds to microseconds: the last unit meaningful to human sensation. Shake past the microsecond to the nanosecond, the picosecond, the femtosecond, the attosecond, the zeptosecond, and you start to wonder if there might be an infinite depth to time, bounded only by our ability to imagine ever-greater numbers, never able to reach a final singularity. The jiffy, for instance, is built of 33 trillion yoctoseconds – one septillionth of a second. To put this in perspective: while there are 10^{18} grains of sand on the planet earth, and 10^{21} stars in the universe, there are 10^{24} yoctoseconds in a second. After this depth into the abyss of time, things get remarkably abstract and less stable – similar to the experience of an atom's life on a gaseous planet. Stability is negotiable.

What is not negotiable, though, is the planck. This is the ground floor of time, the smallest time measurement that will ever be possible. There are 10^{44} plancks in a second – or the number of stars in the universe multiplied by the number of grains of sand on the planet earth. This is not the smallest measure of time meaningful to humans; it is far too small to be meaningful. This has atomic implications and quantum consequences. The planck is the quantum of time. Frozen, the actual porousness of matter would be revealed. Consider a simple fan. When it is turned on, the blades blur and create a solid presence (sped up fast enough, they would be the equivalent of a solid). When the machine stops, though, you can see the empty space between the blades. This is how atoms and their constituent parts create the illusion of solidity. Blades on a fan may take up to half the space of their circle, but the atoms that make us material occupy less than one percent of the body. Without the movement, locked in an irreducible instant, perched upon a single planck, the feel of all material would alter. Without the charge of atoms, gravity would dissipate (not disappear). Were you to move freely in that frozen moment, your strength would increase by multiples of thousands. Movement would never tire you. Your strength would never sag. Moving back and forth between the second and the planck would be an epic journey, in the original sense of the term.

Imagine your first day with this power. You stop time, descend into the frozen moment, and appear across town at a friend's house. You spend your first morning playing practical jokes throughout Toronto. Moving objects – pens, fruits, cushions – until you grow more adventurous and extend the experiment. Your friend is already giving you a slightly terrified look as you laugh at the fridge appearing and disappearing, at the seemingly random encounter of strange objects in the living room. For them, it is to experience a mind completely unhinged, framed only by your dislocated laughter. Was that a tiger? Was that a pile of gold bars? Was that their parents? They recoil from you, the obvious source of the madness. They have to, and you realize your immaturity now. This isn't the power of tricks; this is the power of gods.

You stop time and walk across the continent. Your strength astounds you, and your endurance is enormous. As you walk, you struggle to come to terms with this new dilemma. As you walk, everything on earth starts to feel smaller. You return to your friend's home, but pause to explore every geography of interest in between. You shoplift food, but are never really hungry. You move through these geographies leaving small markers of inexplicable absence: store inventory that doesn't add up, gas subtracted from stations, the odd luxury vanished, a missing car, a little less Scotch.

You know that your effect will linger in those places that will struggle to reconcile the missing goods once time resumes. Jobs will be lost, trust shattered. "I just..." people will start to say, before self-doubt and accusation floods in.

Walking impossible distances, you sometimes forget to breathe, but your body doesn't seem to mind. You are like a ghost and a hulk combined: an ethereal monstrosity. You are outside of biological pressures, markers of decay. Still, you carry a bottle of Domaine de la Romanée-Conti, captured from an upscale liquor mart in California. You don't justify these thefts anymore because you imagine yourself preternaturally removed from the human economy. When you make it home, you have completely lost any meaning of time (the sun does not move in the sky, only you across each horizon).

You sit down across from your friend for a moment before restarting time. You have grown sanguine and serene about your powers, but she will still be startled. You look at the bottle as a cheap trick, but it will make a point. So you resume time and hope to convince her without jarring her into histrionics.

"What's happening?" she pleads. "I keep seeing things. This is insane. I'm going crazy."

You realize that you forgot to return the tiger. From her perspective, it just disappears. She shakes her head and clicks her tongue.

"I'm not sure how to explain. I've discovered a place between the plancks of time and I can go there. Or maybe it is in the plancks, or on the plancks. It's hard to imagine."

"So, what are you, a magician or a time traveller? I thought these were all tricks."

"Not tricks, no, these things are quite real. Do you remember that summer on Lake Joseph? There was a day when we were sprawled out on the dock, soaking up sunshine. A motorboat slowed, do you remember? It nearly cut its engine as it came near. And you looked and then nudged me and said, 'Look!'"

"Mick Jagger."

"Yeah, it was Jagger and his wife or girlfriend, the one who married the French president. And he was kind of showing off for her, smiling, and waved to us when you screamed."

"Yeah. Can you take us back there?"

"No. But do you remember just as the boat passed, we saw a man rise from the backseat that we hadn't seen?"

"Keith Richards."

"Keith Richards. He just kind of looked at us from a place far off in the universe, like he was completely outside of the world. We laughed about it then."

"He is the only living cast member of Body Worlds."

"That place. That place where he goes is where I go."

"I would give all that I am to be unchained to Time."

You look perplexed. "What's that?"

"Shelley. It's just an old quote from Shelley about a friend who died. Keats."

You realize that Shelley is a better analogy than Keith Richards, especially in light of the monster you feel has been unleashed with your power.

"But I haven't died. It's not into death I go, but down into the moment. It's Zen without any of the work."

"Awakened from the dream of life."

"It feels like that. It really does."

She asks you to show her, and you do. She blinks into China. Blinks into Moscow. Blinks into Cuba. A communist tour of the world in under five seconds. She is naturally astounded.

"Did that really happen?"

"Yes." You point to a small pile of trinkets you collected on the way.

She picks up a Mao bobblehead. "How long did it take you?"

"I don't know. It's hard to say. Maybe a year, maybe more. That's what I mean by unhinged."

You watch your friend tremble as she wrestles with this new thought of you, what you might have done in that year. You aren't feeling as earnest anymore.

"Have you told anyone?"

"No."

"Don't."

"You wouldn't know if I did." You pause. "And I might need help…thinking through this. It's a lot to bear. The temptations."

"Let me help," she says rather quickly.

"I was thinking…" you let your voice trail off. It is still resonating in the air when you return with the Dalai Lama. "…something more along these lines."

"Cute," she says, concerned.

The poor man is flustered and you can't get anything from him, so you take him back to New York. Before you return him, though, you pause for a moment on the roof above his hotel. This time he is less perplexed (he has grown accustomed to New York roofs). You tell him about the plancks of time and he seems to understand. He tells a story about the Buddha's experience of nirvana. This is what you wanted. You ask him if there is anything he wants, anything you can do for him.

"Oh, no!" he laughs.

"What about China out of Tibet?"

"No, no, no," he waves, smiling at the naiveté of the thought. "They have to go when they are ready. They will go on their own."

This disappoints you, and when you return home, you compensate by installing a gorgeous swimming pool in her backyard. You restart time and call out to her.

"So this is where you've got to, these past seconds. I was worried you were gone. Thanks for the pool."

"I was."

She strips down and dives in naked. You stop time and swim around her body caught in the air. You can feel that things have changed between you. If you are a gay man or a straight woman, she is already inviting you into the intimacy of indulging in a complex fantasy. If you are a straight man or a lesbian, she is inviting you into a *triste érotique* with time. Something has changed, though, and you pause, floating beneath her body. You climb out of the pool and restart time.

"Where are you?" she cries. "Fuck, I'm not going to get used to that." You both laugh, and she starts talking about your power in environmental terms – moving a mountain, rerouting a river. She has always wanted a mountain, she says, right there. You haven't quite decided what you want to do with it, so you humour her, indulge this play of landscapes.

"How about a simple bouquet to start?" as you hand her the most gorgeous arrangement ever assembled. You can tell that she wants to join you between the plancks, she tells you as much, but you don't know how. You offer to try, and pull her close.

This time, when you stop time, she is there on the other side with you. Inside the moment. Free moving. You laugh to hide the fact that you aren't sure how you feel, as she explores and experiments with the shocking freedom of living in the moment. The near weightlessness, the serene airiness of all the things in the world. You go to Wonderland for a while, then Disney, until the rides are no longer amusing.

"I guess we can't sail to Europe," she says, thinking of Paris. You can tell she is still thinking of herself within time. You tell her various methods. She agrees that it would be useful to learn how to fly. You travel round the world, moving with indulgent leisure through the silent earth. You walk the African savannahs until you come across a den of lions curled in upon each other. The two of you lie down with them, and roll in their thick furs, the only living humans on the planet. You make love on a bed of sleeping lions, because it is the most appropriate thing to do. We have time to figure it out, you laugh. But you don't.

Things fall apart quickly. You've complicated your relationship. Your lack of ambition with your powers, your hesitation, is swamped by her incredible desire to intervene in world affairs. It annoys you that she is behaving as if this is her one opportunity to set things right, though you know it is true. You try to argue with her that you are above that now, you float above the ways of the world in a quiet and lonely freedom. We are the shadows beneath eternity's veil, you decry with half-hearted conviction – you know that only you belong here, but her presence is a gift. A gift to you! She doesn't understand that.

"You would dare to live alone, isolated?" she asks.

"Age cannot destroy me now. Here, at last."

But she is not yet drawn toward the calm endurance of the shadow realm. How could she be? She remains just a visitor. This moment between the plancks is proof of the fragility of governments, human affairs. She is imagining a divine intervention, set on earthly effects, and this desire gives you a chill. You echo the words of the Dalai Lama about self and will and volition, Zen without the work, the necessity of failure, but she has cast her imagination too deep into the waters of affect.

"We can change things," she says. "We can legislate change, move like unseen powers among the people of the entire world. Bring grace, bring peace. We can do this! We have a responsibility, like a debt to this moment. I couldn't live with myself if we didn't at least try to level the field some."

You gradually convince her to return to her house, on various pretenses. This welling ambition in her unsettles you, though you aren't sure why. It seems to open up an enormous pit of darkness. A dream has the power to poison, and already her dreaming has poisoned your wild dissolving bliss.

In her home, you pull her close and give her a long, lingering kiss. You can feel her ambition electric through her skin. She can feel your withdrawal. You break apart. Everything is revealed in a series of quick glances.

"Don't," she says. "Don't."

"I'm sorry," you offer meekly. "We can't fix the future."

You restart time with a sigh, but unexpectedly she simply disappears. Sinking inside, you realize that she did not make the leap. You were not holding her, she let go or you did; her imprint still remains impressed on your skin, your skin darkens from the white of her touch.

You panic. You stop time again, but she is gone. The difference between one planck of time and the next one is infinity (in fact, all the stars in the universe multiplied by all the grains of sands on the planet earth; infinities). She remains trapped forever where you brought her. You sit down, feeling a hollowness that stops your breath. You marvel at your mistake, your foolishness, your forgetfulness. You let it all slip away. All the memories of your time in that planck, one voluminous (endless if you can't end it) moment, cycles through your mind. You return to the thought of making love on the bed of lions. Was it worth it? It was, you decide, the tipping point in latent conflicts. It was the failed test of the limits of your power. You still don't know how much you can do, but you know now one line you cannot cross. The past cannot be accessed. Some mistakes cannot be corrected.

You start to come around to the burden of your guilt. It is done and cannot be undone. You vow to build her a mountain. You stand up and walk toward the windows at the back of the house, as if to begin the planning and imagining of that momentous task. On the table, though, you notice a finely gilded card that bears your name in finely wrought ink.

"Hey you," it reads intimately.

"I left something for you in the fridge. Don't drop it.
With a forgiving love,
Connie."

Your eyes well up as you follow the curl of her hand-writing, and picture the terrible isolation in which she wrote this note. You grip it tightly as you walk toward the fridge, which you find empty but for a bottle of Domaine de la Romanée-Conti. There are two glasses. Wistfully, you pull them out, let one touch your lip. Don't drop it, you think. You won't.

You fill your glass with the wine and turn around to face a spectacle beyond your ability to render. The entire wall has been replaced with a window of a type you can't recognize. It is thin, porous almost, like the glass wall is itself alive and rendering what it displays. You half feel like you are already outside. The scene, the outside, is even more disturbing than this impossible glass. Your small if elegant swimming pool remains, but beyond and surrounding it, the land cuts away into the sheer cliffs of an enormous canyon that sweeps away beyond your sightlines. It drops into a seething darkness. Beyond this canyon is a mountain that makes Mount Fuji look subtle. You drop the bottle.

Out in front of the house, the entire suburban street has been transformed into a glimmering boulevard built out of all your childhood fantasies. Can you imagine the spectacle of phantom lampposts, statuesque monoliths and a wide expanse of bejewelled walkway? It all leads in one direction, which route you passively follow. There is no trace of the suburb, and you start to feel that it would make no difference if you started time or not. This is an encapsulated jewel-encrusted space. At the end of the street is an architectural wonder of a style you cannot recognize. It isn't futuristic or neo-primitive – it is merely...alien. You walk up the capacious steps, only gradually realizing the presence of an advanced technology that has been monitoring you all along.

"I know you're watching me," you holler.

A clean mechinic voice, with faint traces of Connie encoded into its digital signature, replies flatly, "Please. Come inside."

Inside the building is a grand welcoming chamber, pointing perfectly toward the moment of your arrival. It has been built for you, you flatter yourself (and it has indeed anticipated your need for flattery). As you step forward, a hologram of Connie appears. She explains that they are using this old technology to help you understand. That she lived for many generations until she experimented with birth technologies and had children. Many of them. It is easier here, she says, lighter and far quicker. She says she used to joke with her granddaughters about the issues you people used to have with abortion. Of course, as this new kind of population spread across the globe, they were compelled to abort the frozen population. At first they called them "sleepers," eventually calling them "stones," eventually calling them something that doesn't translate. Eventually, they stopped referring to them at all. Except for you, she says. You play a special role in all of this. She admitted aborting felt a bit like smashing fine sculpture. You had to feel for the sculptor, she says.

She speaks of her brood in terms of generations, as in gen7 or gen12, and you are astonished to hear the range of numbers she discusses, and the geographies they claimed, even invented. "I don't know where that is," you say more than once. "You wouldn't," is all she offers. "What killed the sleepers?" the young would ask. "They were frozen" became the adopted metaphor. Eventually only small groups of the curious would ask at all. Humans have receded into our primitive past. It's hard to explain, she says, that people once died of time. Even I sometimes forget what time meant or felt like, she says. The hologram of Connie starts to crackle and hardens into a real body. She is standing right in front of you as if herself.

"Now that you've seen this much, you are ready for another dose of the truth. I was alone. Alone for a long, long time. I don't know, thousands of years, more, I suppose. It is impossible to judge such things. All alone. I went through many changes. The young ones tell stories of the dynasties of my moods and my projects."

"It was only a moment for me," you whisper.

"Every moment is eternity when you dwell there. I learned enough to advance your technologies until I had no more use for your people's knowledge, your people. I collected them all and terminated them when I realized what was at stake. I can live anywhere in the universe. I need nothing. Since I began breeding, we have learned enough to leave the planet. It doesn't matter if I tell you where. You will never be able to return to our planck, though you might seek us out to discover what became of us. Me. We have created spectacles that you could not comprehend. And I mean that literally. We have expanded the number of our senses, expanded their range, expanded the capacity and speed of our brains. Our bodies achieved a sublime velocity when we replaced our functionless blood with light. It is hard to explain to you all that we have become."

"What are you?"

"Some of the youngest speak of me as the daughter of the end. What you see before you, though, is simply printed matter. A printed version of what you remember. People were already printing toys and houses when you left me. We've learned a lot about matter since then, even though matter in motion, the idea of atoms moving, is a theory my young struggled hard and long to imagine. But this me, this printed me, will still be here when you start time again."

"Where are you?"

"It doesn't matter. What matters is that we've gone. We've decided to allow the planet to recreate itself. You are the last one here. Eventually, you will want to restart time. When that happens, the animals will flourish. We have come to value the diversity of animals on earth far more than human contributions. It is a far more barren universe than you might hope. In any event, our thinking, as it is, circles around the prospect of the restart of time. We call it the beginning and we have prepared the earth well for it. When you do it, of course, is entirely up to you. As you can imagine, you fulfill all the needs we have for a god. Not you, exactly, but your power."

"There's nothing left."

"That's not exactly true. You have the choice. You can start it up again and let yourself die, or you can set to find us. We have reached the point where it doesn't matter to us whether time starts or not. We have solved that problem."

A horror creeps over you. You run from the chamber, run back home, through to the edge of the cliff before the endless canyon. It is a dark mass at the bottom. When you climb down, you realize the darkness is the broken remains of humanity. Cut down like abandoned husks. This is how the earth restarts itself, you think. This is the myth of the flood. The fertile ground will decompose and life will start again.

You look up in the sky and see the pale day moon. She has carved into it a perfect likeness of your face. You realize that it will blur and fade by the time of the next civilization. They will grow up with ghostly legends of what lies beyond. You set to work.

George McWhirter

SISTERS IN SPADES

Sister Felicitas scolds me. Usually, it is my bad calculus or lab book that gets it; this time, it's taking a spade from where it leans against what was the gardener's lodge, but which now serves as the school chemistry lab. The men who do the garden don't live-in anymore.

I can't believe Sister Felicitas has taken the spade from me so daintily. Outdoors, the gym-and-chem teacher grabs everything like a bat, but inside she is otherwise. This is the inside Sister, who handles the spade as she does tetrameters, beakers and slender vials to be stored in the lab fridges.

After resting the spade back against the wall, Sister Felicitas brushes her grey cardigan and pleated grey skirt.

"But why does he leave it here?" I ask.

"Who's he?"

"The gardener."

"Have you been watching one of the labourers…have you some arrangement attached to this spade?"

The wood on the grip has a leathery glaze from the hands that use it.

"Sister Felicitas, would I ask *you* why the gardener leaves it here, if *I* had anything to do with him?"

I pose the point, logically, like the nuns teach us to. I get no answer.

"Should it not be in the tool shed – out of the weather?" I wallow in saying weather, the Irish way, meaning rain.

"I caught sight of him," I say, choosing my words. "He wears leggings made out of old sacks, tied round his shins." Like a poor man's puttees, I think, but don't say.

"You are…if I remember rightly…a Waterston?"

All St. Ursa's girls are addressed by surnames, but I'm stumped at once by her "a," which puts me in my place through the Waterston collective.

"You know fine well I am, Sister Felicitas."

"And sent back."

I think Sister Felicitas refers to placement, my being put back a year into Fifth Form when I came from Mississauga to St. Ursa's in Ireland.

"What's your meaning, Sister?"

"Sent back to your old home," Sister Felicitas frowns. "The Waterstons are not supposed to touch anything to do with the property. Keep in touch, and your family has, but the property is to be left alone. Everything in the garden has its place, and it's not for you to choose where they go any more. How did you happen to see this…gardener?"

I point up to the window that looks down from our attic dorm.

"From our room."

"Then, you must be moved. We can't have our girls watching young men going about their work. Especially, a Waterston."

Once again, my curse of being a Waterston in the town of Waterston, in what was Waterston Hall. As bad as being the head teacher's daughter. Extra severity seeps into the Sisters' voices when they mention any deficit in my studies or appearance. Like some form of fat, I feel debilitated by Waterston money. My father did tell me to dig into my schoolwork, not our history. But said as if Dad insinuated I should.

In bed I often do a rewind mind-run on the toboggan down the slope from the back of our Mississauga house to the Credit River. In Mississauga, Ontario, I fill the slope with school friends to crowd out whatever my father, grand-mother and great-grandmother stare at there, on the slope from our house down to the Credit River.

I have had this luxury of Waterston women to advise and the family business to prepare me. Rosheen Waterston, my great-grandmother, filed the first records and did searches for guests at the Toronto hub. The Waterstons have always run Lineage Hotels, which operate not unlike the Mormon Centre in Salt Lake City with its worldwide family informa-tion and data base. This feature keeps Waterston Hotels run-ning as continuous conference and research centres. But my father still speaks to my grandmothers and my mother about me as if I'm not there – even before I'm not there.

"Can she bear to be on her own with only memories of us to keep her company?"

"Memories are a man's distraction, but woman's daily bread. In any case, it's our trade," my grandmother harrumphs at him, and my mother won't even look up at my father from the chair where she sits, reading *Chatelaine*.

I quote her. "She abhors his absurd mix of sentimentality and trepidation at his decision to return his daughter to the fold, but then she only married into the Waterstons."

They gather in the kitchen, like it's their debating chamber. Kessie, the cook, uses a wooden spoon, a pot or a pan like a gavel when discussion gets in the way of their eating or her cooking.

They settle my switching schools over a seafood sauce and pasta-draining session. "The Grey Nuns will take care of her."

"The Grey Nuns?" I ask.

"Charity begins at home, in our case, our old home," I am informed.

I learn Waterston Hall was a gift to the Grey Nuns in Ireland, and Waterston Hall is now St. Ursa's School, where the nuns shall pass the benefit of their wisdom and instruction on to me. Amen.

"Okay, I agree to a good Catholic education, and to live without a friend in the world." Neither relieved nor pleased, they peer at me like I am one of Kessie's pots and colanders she has struck with her wooden spoon.

In Mississauga I would be going into Grade 12 after the summer break; at St. Ursa's I'm in Fifth Form. Put back and prickly as a pincushion about it, I badger to Sister Felicitas in Chemistry over my top mark for my lab book. "Shows I should be in the Sixth Form," I tell her.

"Don't feel that you are behind, Jean. The Irish are always ahead of themselves in their educational standards because of their reputation for being backward, but then, the Irish always see their way forward by looking back."

"Sounds like everything slips into reverse, here! Even common sense," I say before I can stop myself.

"You are only going back a year, one of the hundreds."

From Waterston, a view of the Boyne lies in the distance. The lawned slope from the school leads into squared fields, clusters of trees and towns, a misty grid and something else of mystery and muddle haunts my heritage: this spade.

"Well, it's back for him when he comes to get it, later?"

I startle Sister Felicitas with this reply.

"How much later?" she snaps.

If the young man props the spade opposite the girl's dorm, he does so for attention, but I don't disclose that I wait at the dorm window till he picks up his spade and takes it into the dark with him. Like a gaffer I keep a time sheet in an exercise book for him: his hours of departure and return. After a night's labour, shaking with exertion and steaming with sweat or dew, he leans on his spade, wraps his fist around the handle, which digs in under his breastbone, like it's giving him a paralyzing punch to the pelvis.

When I gently open the window, I hear the same thing every night: "'Taint no way enuf. Nine hours solid, and bad as ever, when I've done. Not'in' where it shud be."

This last night, before the Sisters move me, I'm down beside him, exercise book and pen in hand, to ask a question.

"Where should everything be?"

"Where it was."

I flinch at this and wonder if he has seen me touch the spade.

"Trenches were easier, Miss." He wipes his hands on his hips. "You're not angry at me, are you?" he asks.

"Should I be?"

"Perhaps not – leastways, y'r' talkin' to me. Nobody else is. Disgusted, are they?"

"I think it best I don't speak for the rest."

"Well, I put in the hours, Miss. Thousands and I'm beat."

"But you haven't given me your name for my records!"

I never knew I could sound so bossy and bold.

"Bowse Cartey. Do you not remember – the only one who volunteered? "

Now, he stalks off on me, giving me the view of his back.

"Volunteered for what?" I call after him.

A letter to my dad gets one from my grandmother back: "*Bowse Cartey joined Sean Redmond's Southern Volunteers in the Great War. He planted perennials, torch lilies, to come back to, and never saw them. Over there in Belgium, mortally wounded, a Grey Nun nursed him on his deathbed, and in a delirium, he proposed to the nun. People on the estate said he might have confused the nun with Cissy Waterston, who would be your great-great-aunt, were she alive. Bowse followed Cissy with his spade held across his shoulder, like a rifle, as if he were honour guard for her special projects to brighten the gardens. The photo of Cissy will let you understand the added confusions for Bowse with you.*

I can see.

Cissy's me with a lovely ruffle collar, running around her neck and all the way down to her waist, *small as a wasp's*, like my grandmother says. *Not Cissy's choice for the photograph, but done to please* her *grandmother. As for the nun, at eighty years of age she finally came over with her order to our gift of Waterston Hall and with this wish from Cartey: for her to visit him where things would look their best.*

They all shook hands at the handing over to become St. Ursa's. My father always said the nun wore a smile when she looked past them all at the garden, and she talked to it, "Tu sembles bien, mais pas heureux – fatigué, comme tous les homme qui travail pour rendre la nature de plus en plus belle dans son lit. Tu est fiel plus longtemps que la mort."

That was the last look she took at anything in this world. Funny old nun, she had been one of the negotiators, responsible for relocating the order after the War.

Which war?

This much leaves me feeling like the Belgian nun: a little light in one hemisphere. *We know whatever is up with him, you will put him straight. You're a Waterston and you're a woman* – end of Granny's letter.

When did I have my family graduation to woman?

Several days after I'm moved, Sister Felicitas says my eyes look unhealthy. They have shadows under them like I boot-polished them to pull on a helmet and play some ridiculous sport. Or go on a night raid.

Will I or won't I tell her?

To my mind the sister is SF. Her initials, and being into science and gymnastics makes Sister Felicitas as fantastic to me as science fiction. If she's not in the lab, she's in the gym or on a court coaching. Maybe Cartey comes to moon over her. Half of the girls do, some in the demurest and some in the dirtiest way, choosing to work out on the exercise benches or the courts till their nipples stick through the blots of sweat on their sports halters and their armpit hair is treated like *the* badge of bravery.

"Has he said anything to you?" Sister Felicitas asks me.

I don't know what to answer, so I quote him: " 'I can't get it right. The place is as bad as ever.' I think that's it, but he mumbles."

"Is that all?"

"No, he said I'm a Waterston. Miss Waterston, actually, and it's all right for me if I keep track of him."

"For you to what?"

"Keep track. Until you moved me, I kept a time sheet of all the times he came and went with his spade in an exercise book."

"Is that so? And he talks like someone who isn't trying to get off with you?"

"Sister Felicitas. He talks like he's an employee and I'm his supervisor."

"Mistress would be a better word. Well, you'll have to give him his marching orders, eventually."

"I will?"

"You're a Waterston, as he said?"

I'm flabbergasted as Sister Felicitas kisses my cheek.

"Time to get these fixed," she says to the bags under my eyes.

Since so many of the pupils at St. Ursa's have parents in business, Small Business Essentials is on the curriculum for the upper-level girls. We don't ever ask, "What about big business?" One girl who did was told, "For big, do the same, only more."

Taking on and laying off, humanely, is introduced, since many of us – the privileged – will be called upon to do it, and therefore are fit subjects for the topic. Once upon a time, we are told, dismissal training would have been for suitors, a specialty of the finishing schools, but the sisters are here to prevent us from cutting people dead and conducting an inhumane and spiritless business.

"For most," Sister Bénédicité tells us, "the hardest lesson is learning when to quit. In an ideal world we would recognize our own incompetence or redundancy. We should see it in our own faces, but that isn't the way it works."

I have the creepy feeling I am the sole object of these weird remarks or someone sitting directly behind me is.

During History, Sister Beatrix reprises the insult to Redmond and the Southern Volunteers. No officers, unable to issue their own orders. They stood in wait for commands to be given by Englishmen, which suited some.

Is that what Cartey waits for?

I see him at the end of the nine-hour night, leaning his head against the chemistry lab wall. He twists his fist on the handle of his spade, like a throttle. He mutters at me or someone, doubles over till the top of his head buries itself in the ivy on the wall. He reaches down and plucks at the sacking around his trouser bottoms, like he's trying to read the few letters that are left there from the brand of sugar it held.

"Well?" he says and turns to look at my exercise book and pen, then my wristwatch. I tap my pen on my exercise book.

"Just say the word."

"You're sacked," I say, experimentally. Then, without a second thought, "Pick up your things and go."

His relief frightens me. It's like lightning.

As for Bowse Cartey's work and enslavement to loyalty, I'd love to find a torch lily he planted, especially when I discover it's a nice name for a red-hot poker, and take it in to Sister Cecilia, who teaches botany and music. But I come across no such thing. The gardens are all low-maintenance. Perhaps it's better so, otherwise Bowse might come back and spend eternity seeing to the torch lilies' welfare.

Madeline Sonik

PUNCTURES

The day I was born, they dug a hole – the kind of deep down deep hole that makes you dizzy when you look inside. I didn't die. Don't know if they were expecting me to. Don't know for certain why they dug the hole. I only know that they never shovelled it in.

My first memories are of women, mothers-to-be, in colourful sacks. Sweet misery lived in their faces and their stomachs grew torturously slow. Then the babies were everywhere – in every house, on every porch step, their flat round faces pushed up against windows, their luminous eyes peeking out of every void.

At eight o'clock, you could hear them screaming, in a jumbled chorus of colic, with aches and appetites, with itches and thirst, a din so loud that nothing could drown it. How they wept. How they carried on. Even the cotton you shoved in your ears held their unhappy howling. Their bellows were blades that scored your skull, and nothing could be done to stop it, until at last you passed from stricken wakefulness to restless sleep. Then, in the morning, when the babies grew quiet, when there might have been calm, in rolled the builders, with saws and hammers, and trucks – with long wooden planks, plasterboard, and sacks of powdered cement. All through the town, there were taps and bangs and the screech of tires spinning in mud, and the babies filling the world with startled, tired sobs.

Bright arrows of sun penetrated our blinds. Our rooms grew hot as ovens, yet we slept from exhaustion, in fretful repose. When we finally woke, there were changes – extended houses, brand new nursery wings. We noticed the deliveries, the cribs, the changing tables, the rocking chairs. Mud hills twisted like monster chocolate kisses, high up into the blue skies. They pushed the city limits with their circumference, pushed the land beyond its natural size. They swallowed forests, ate animals, sucked in chain-link fences.

Mountains of mud bulged in the backyard of each expanding home and the babies took to their peaks, crawling and stumbling, teetering at their tops. From my window I could see them, shiny with mud, grinning and frowning, tumbling and rolling. I could see them up there, and I could also see their mothers on the ground, in those sacks, exhausted and unable to shriek, because fatigue had sealed their mouths with apathy. There were babies just walking, and crawlers and creepers. There were bald babies and hairy babies, babies who would strip off their clothing and whimper when the sun would dry the mud on their flesh. I could see babies wobbling at the tops of the mountains, losing their balance, toppling out of sight. "Poor babies," I'd think, looking at the places they'd been, looking at their sweet miserable mothers, who were helpless in the clutches of their tedious, colourful gowns.

The mountains had been growing for such a long time that no one knew what was beyond them anymore. We hoped for a better world – but no one knew where the fallen had vanished, and there wasn't enough time in the day between our shattered waking and paralyzed sleep to climb to the tops of those mountains and see.

In those hot summer months, after the babies started vanishing, a new sound accompanied their cries. It started as an eerie hum in the evening that rose to a jagged crescendo. I wondered if perhaps it was the sound of the fallen, if perhaps the fallen were calling back, an echo, a memory, if somewhere out there they were waiting, and I tried to imagine them whole. I tried to imagine their chubby, trusting bodies and their inquisitive, puckered smiles. I held them in my mind and saw them as they had been: blinking their wide, glassy eyes in troubled confusion. I saw them in their muddy shrouds, their sagging diapers, their distress, and before them I envisioned a long weathered path, up the mountains, bringing them home. It was possible that such a path could exist, I told myself, and so expectant, waited, listening to the hum and its ever-increasing swell. I was certain that soon they would find their way back, but before summer ended the hum turned into a buzz, and droves of wasps, not babies, ascended the mountains' tops. They soared and spun high in the sky and dipped down to the ground, collecting miniature measures of mud. They rolled these parcels into balls, and carried them to houses, to playground jungle gyms, to trees, to telephone poles. They smashed the balls with their heads, moulded the mud into long thin artistic tubes. Other insects grew jealous. Other insects picked at the mud as well, but the wasps pushed themselves into nail holes, they lowered themselves into hollow plant stems, they buried themselves beneath the dark, rich mud of the mountains and hauled it up into the heavens to make their homes. Their buzz became a solid drone, constant as stone. From my window, I watched the wasps coming and going and the babies still tottering and crawling up the slippery slopes – their tiny hands extending toward the creatures, their bright little faces turning crimson at the sight. The wasps thrust stingers into soft baby flesh, and the babies in grieving consternation, with their little bow mouths, incredulous and turning upside down toward the mud, reeled and dropped like lead-bottomed dolls over the peaks and into the abyss.

All the while below, their mothers melted in the heat of summer, fanning themselves with parenting magazines and tight, white disposable diapers – and all the while below, the builders continued building, extending, improving. The truck drivers continued delivering. Everyone's faces were portraits of emptiness, and I didn't like to see, but I couldn't stop from watching. "There goes another baby," I'd think, and the eerie drone of wasps grew louder.

Exterminators came in goggles and white zip-up suits. They slung tanks of pesticide over their backs, and dusted every square inch of mud, but it didn't seem to matter what they did: the wasps wouldn't go away. Everywhere you looked now, you'd see them weaving invisible highways in the air, building nests and stuffing them with victim mites.

Some of the nests resembled intricate clay pots, others stunningly hewn flutes. The nests increased with manic rapidity. The drone reverberated to a roar. The mud mountains grew higher and higher, and our town caught every single echo. When the babies sobbed, the roar was thunderous, as if the wasps in restless agitation had decided they would never be outdone. The noise was unthinkable and gargantuan. At eight, as I lay on my bed, my eyes reflexively drilled holes in the ceiling for release – the moan and blubber of babies, the torrential downpour of wasps. I shoved and adjusted rubber and cotton, I pulled padded boxes over my ears, I crammed my head into the depths of an insulated bucket, and, finally, was rewarded with oblivion.

When I heard the piping from beyond the mountains a week later, I no longer thought of a better world. I no longer thought of the fallen with their glassy baby gazes or a path that might bring them home. I thought only of the mud, and the hole that was dug on the day I was born, and wondered what the outcome would be.

In retrospect, it seems inevitable – that gliding and plunging, as they came in flocks over the mountains snapping wasps in their beaks. I was standing at the window, listening to the roar and watching the babies on the mountains. I was saying, "Poor baby, poor baby" when suddenly, in a burst of colour and light, thousands of swallows, piping and whistling, cheeping and chattering, surged, it seemed, in all different directions over the mountain and into our town.

The babies on the mountain stopped climbing and crawling, their round little faces twisted up toward the clouds; even those warbling in the throes of pain lifted their eyes to heaven and watched the graceful long-tailed swallows diving and darting like streamers in the air. They hovered over the mountains, their wings straight above their backs. They dipped their dainty bills into the mountain, then streaked off to houses and trees, to water towers and electrical poles, depositing pellets of mud. In five days, not one eave was without a nest. In fourteen, their nests were visible on plant pots and lawn ornaments. Patio tables swelled with mud tumours; dark excrescences formed on abandoned park benches, gourds of mud thickened and pouched on every glistening satellite dish.

Nests filled with oyster-white eggs. Curious baby eyes gazed. Curious baby hands grabbed. And then, what a godforsaken commotion there was. Swallows and babies, babies and swallows, all of them screaming and thrashing.

The babies got the worst of it, though. Blood ran down their cheeks like jam. They were stung by the wasps the swallows didn't eat, pushed over the tops of the mountains by their own despair. Their mothers fanned themselves, stomachs protruding, sweat falling and marking their swelling gowns. In sixteen days, the swallow eggs were nestlings, raucous and insatiable. The town was teeming with life. At eight o'clock, the racket was unendurable: babies, wasps, swallows, nestlings and the mountains now, so much larger than they'd been, collecting every whisper and throwing it back, like voices from a well.

If we fell asleep, we didn't know. If we stayed awake, we couldn't tell. Days and nights, nights and days, whirling together with teeming life, with mud and construction. Noise ate noise, buzz ate birdsong, howl ate howl, until all that was left in our town was one drawn-out chaotic cry – the scream of mud enlivened.

I'd given up thinking of the fallen. I stopped pondering the hole. I found it difficult to hope. "What is the sound of lost hope?" I wondered. A hum, a chirp, a cry? I caught myself thinking of this often, thinking of this every day as I watched the babies teetering on mountains, as I watched them falling. "Poor babies," I'd think, "Poor babies," I'd say. "What is the sound of lost hope?" And although I didn't know, I believed it might be the sound I heard next.

I wanted to tell someone, to say something, but I held my tongue. I held my tongue and in a week, above the raucous cacophony, there came a sharp and lucid "ping." "What made a noise like that?" I wondered. It sounded like a sack breaking. "What makes a sound like that?" I asked myself, and thought that others in the town must be asking this too. Then there was a rush and rumble, a whoosh. I got out of bed and looked through the window. The babies! The mountains! They were all spilling down into the vale. Sludge washing over everything. Wasps and swallows sinking like pebbles in a stream. Muck pounding over houses and machines, muck knocking everything down and leaving nothing.

I held my tongue and watched the babies in a tumultuous heap flapping their little arms and kicking their feet, until they grew weak and drifted. I held my tongue, until the mountains were levelled and the babies sank, and there was such a silence I could hear myself breathe. Then I climbed out of my window, stepped into the thick black mire and began fishing. I could feel the mud oozing up past my knees, over my thighs. How would I ever be able to clean all the babies? How would I ever be able to wash this away? I sank to my hips before I saw the place of the hole. The mud had covered it, slick and even – fresh as a newborn's flesh, and before I retrieved the first little corpse, a thunderous laugh burst from my mouth and filled the great unrelenting void. It was the mud that brought the laughter, the mud that filled the hole, and suddenly, with its dirty certainty, convinced me that nothing I had ever cared about had ever been of any consequence.

Leon Rooke

SLAIN BY
A MADMAN

He was. He was slain by a madman. He was slain once all over and the madman wasn't done and did him a second time, top to bottom. I won't say it was not deserved. We all of us might have slain him, if we'd known we could get away with it. The whole town contemplated the act a thousand times, daylight through dark. This way, that way, which way ever we could think.

A Day Pass! They let him out on a Day Pass. Who could have imagined such! That institution was asking for trouble. And where does he go on this Day Pass? He comes here. Of course he does. He comes home.

So the actual hard-nosed slaying of him by the madman brought some easement to the local situation. But process and accomplishment are two different experiences is what I am saying. Like they are hardly even related. Like you have three sisters totally in disagreement as to character and dimension, and their mother in far orbit and the father so different from those others he's hardly worth mentioning.

The madman, who can talk a blue streak when he wants to, isn't saying much. What he said, in a calm voice chilling to behold, was he didn't do it. "Affliction's giant foot is ever stomping down," he said. "You want to know what marks humankind? That foot. The giant behemoth." The next second he clammed up. "Now I'm going silent as the little lamb who made me" were his actual words to the authorities, by which I mean me. I'm the law around here. Running a pretty tight ship. Such is what I told this person when she came in, looking all fidgety and run down – *strung out!* – claiming the madman could not, could not, *could not possibly!* – be the guilty party.

Did I know at that point she was the madman's sweetheart? No, I did not.

What I said was, "Delores, dear little sister, why in God's name are you here?"

She said, "Because the party you've got locked up back there could not possibly be the guilty party."

I laughed. Delores is always eager-beaver about something.

"Why not?" I said.

"On account of his having been in my arms at The Only Motel when said deed was said to have been accomplished." She sat right down in my chair, in that thigh-high red pokey-dot dress, saying this. Drinking this Slurpee drink thing through a straw. "He may well be a madman," she said, "and I suppose he is in the minds of some thwarted, decomposing individuals, but no way would he pass up a good time with me to wreak what havoc you say he wrought on that other fella."

I said, "Now, come on."

She said, "You come on."

I said, "Honey, you are a lying cockroach. At the time of the deed you were teaching your six-year-olds how to hop, skip and jump, and not at no motel."

She said, "Every Wednesday at 2 p.m. for the past two years I been hopping on my bike and meeting my madman at The Only Motel. I give my little serpents the *Bad Frog* book to play out."

"Not the *Bad Frog*!"

"People wanting to git that book banned left town. It's back on the curriculum, hot as potatoes."

"Damn," I said.

She scowled. She hated cussing.

I said, "All right. You can go on home now. But don't say nothing to your mother about no motel."

"Oh, poor mother! It's her wash day," she said.

She went.

But first she said, "I know my man is no Goody Two-Shoes and that he seduced a nun in the long ago. It's jealousy is what it is. All you randy he-hunks want to seduce a nun. Don't try telling me different."

"Now, hold your horses," I said.

"He is the apple of my eye, my solace in the crippling storm, and I am up to here with certain people casting aspersions on his character. Just because he once made out with a dumb nun."

She sliced a hand up by her chin, saying that. The little pokey-dots bounced all over.

Then she went.

❧

I sat a long time mulling over her words. He-hunk? But "havoc wrought upon *that other fella*" gave me pause. Did she not know this *other fella* bore her identical name? That, biologically speaking, he was family? Or was she, like the rest of us, bound to deny such until our dying day?

Here he came on his Day Pass. Spotted the instant he steps off the bus. Baggy suit. Emaciated. Good. May he expire on the spot, we thought. Shoot him. Knife him. Next he's seen peering into the new Subway. He's taking gauge of changes since his departure ages ago. What is that he is carrying in the left hand? Is that a gasoline can? Is that a cigarette between his lips? Yes.

Yes yes yes.

❧

I went, too. I got the lights spinning and the siren churning and I juiced right over. I went to The Only Motel.

A short minute before arriving I passed the family ruins and the glistening enmity of Mink Lake. How I hated that lake. But the road was straight and I could close my eyes.

A toxic wasteland, the sky ever-smoking black above it.

A poetic line occurred to me: *May the tears of ravaged angels cleanse my cheeks.*

❧

"Explain your needs," Ms. Fixit said to me. Ms. Fixit, what I call her, is one of three sisters running the place. She said, "It's not Tuesday, why are you here?" She said, "Your usual room is occupied and, anyway, Vivian is in Buffalo.

"Shopping," she said.

"You look terrible," she said. "You need a good mud-pack ointment on that flesh."

Vivian is one of the three sisters. She doesn't get along that well with the other two. What I say to that is who can.

Me and Vivian, to make no bones about it, have a thing going. She was supposed to keep her trap shut about it, but, women, what can you say?

"She's buying a new mattress," sister Fixit said. "A new man, a new mattress. Every time. It sure beats me."

"Never mind that," I said. "I seek confirmation on a love tryst involving the madman and a certain redhead named—"

"Yes, yes, yes!" is what I got in return. "I can set my clock by that pair. Dee zips in on that yellow bike, he zooms in on that red truck. Then you don't hear a peep from in there until the six o'clock news."

"Damn," I said.

"You might as well face it. Those two are practically wed."

"No way am I welcoming another madman into the family."

"Another would hardly be noticed," she said.

"Now hold on."

"You hold on."

Her hands and hips were covered in mud. So, too, the naked feet and in her hair.

Smoke was rising from a barrel out back. "What are you burning out there?" I asked.

"Your bed sheets?" Ms. Fixit said. She was a smart-mouthed, big-knuckled woman known far and wide. The black folds of history had not obscured her light. To hear her tell it. It seemed to me the flesh darkened under her eyes each time she spoke to me. I could remember holding her down when we were little. Maybe she remembered, too. Although Vivian said neither of her sisters remembered last week. You never know. I had held her down and got in a good bite on her neck. Then everybody else had piled on. The adults hadn't minded. They thought we were having fun. What she had said was I had a teensy weenie and only fruitcakes would ever look at me. She deserved those bites.

This, of course, was before the mayhem.

"Where's Marlene?" I asked. Marlene was third in the sister trio and way older. Miss Moneybags, they called her, on account of her being the bookkeeper and payroll mistress and hard-nosed tyrant yard-boss who every day strode about in logging boots with her white mane flying.

"In town getting her shots," I was told.

Shots?

"Yes, shots, by God. One shoots off to Buffalo to buy a mattress, the other shoots into town to get her fanny pumped up with shots. Who, by God, is left here to do all the work?" She went red in the face, saying that.

"Well," I said, "you'd best get at it."

"I don't like your tone," she said. "I don't like your tone one teensy bit."

The Only Motel dogs were snarling in a distant field.

"Those dogs," I said.

She said, "Yep. Dogs." And strode off to the lean-to where she makes her mud pots. Not mud, I've been told, but clay from the good earth. Sometimes, when they are talking to each other, you see the three sisters out there shovelling ivory-tinted clay into buckets, milky lumps from the high walls of the small stream quietly flowing behind The Only Motel. Mink Lake the wellspring. My water, in other words. It has taken, I'm told, ten thousand years for that clay to form. They slip and slide, they tumble, they swat at each other. Always one or the other, sooner or later, will throw down her shovel and crawl miserably from the ditch, shouting nastiness at the others and at any lodger who chances to be on hand.

At times, the water in that stream runs the colour of blood, who knows why. Blood shades the favoured glaze.

"This is preliterate clay!" storms Viv, when in one of her fits. "This is pre-agriculture clay! This clay predates the Age of Reason by thirty thousand years! All we needed was a big bonfire! While we're at it, throw in a virgin child, why not!"

"Oh, come on."

"You come on."

❧

Way off there, in a grove of warped trees, sits the parental home, parents abiding mysteriously within, a chain fence in surround of this, No Trespassing signs dotting your every step. Keep Out Keep Out. Mind the dogs.

"They are perfectly normal," Viv has said. "You ought not broadcast these erroneous details."

Erroneous, my word! Meanwhile, drone planes fly invisibly overhead. Our nation's on the watch.

They've got suspicions, too, about those nuns.

Sisters and parents had been visiting the day hell broke loose. Dinner! Ice cream! Dee, playing in a sandbox – chasing a cow? – had been spared. She was what? Two? I was eight. Nine? Did I yet know my arithmetic tables? No I didn't.

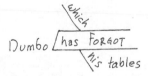

Is that right? In this backwoods hole, before the nuns, did we diagram a sentence that way? Yes we did.

❦

It was a woman's shoe the dogs were arguing over. A black pump. Well, once black. Now it was mostly slobber. Slime. Grit. One dog had the toe, the other the heel. They were pulling and twisting, having a dandy time. What that shoe reminded me of was the madman's befouled nun. In her

nunnery period she had worn a man's black, clumpy shoe.
My men had done a lot of snooping on that nun. We
knew everything about her except why she'd give up her
virtue to a madman. Although that did, looked at in a certain way, make sense. She was still around, that nun. She
had wanted to marry the madman back then, and have his
children. She could be very specific about it, if you ran
into her at the Easy-Go or the Drugs. "By God, I still do,"
she'd say. "I'd toss up Chuck and my current crop of sweet
babies for five minutes with that madman." Chuck, he
pulls on his suspenders, he laughs. "My simple tool," she
calls Chuck.

Once, I was eating a footlong at our splendid new
Subway and her boss shoves into my booth. I'm looking at
his white collar the whole time he's talking to me. Finally I
have to ask him, "How do you birds keep those white collars so clean? Never a smudge. Nothing. Me, a dirt collar-
ring the minute I don a shirt." He looks surprised. "Why,
my Lord, my flock sees to that! My nuns! Goodness gra-
cious me!"

Then he smiles, he says, "Or maybe we don't sweat."

Next, the smile deepens and he says, "Or if we do, it's
the sweat of Christ reminding us that divinity and hard
work are soul-brothers making our day."

What he'd been complaining about prior to that was his
shrinking population. He'd lost three nuns – "*Three!*" – in
the past year. What was it? Was it the air people breathed in
this town? Was it creeping socialist criminalization of a dis-
engaged citizenry? Was there a sex club afoot, their whole

goal the claiming of his nuns? "I tell no lie, they catch sight of the madman, they go giddy. They waddle about like cracked eggs. They'd die to ride in his truck."

What could I say? The madman's a handful. He's no picnic.

I thought about having me a slug from the bottle in the glove compartment when I got back to the cruiser.

I could see Ms. Fixit working at her wheel was giving me long looks. The "V" in the neon over The Only Motel office was blinking. It had been blinking for about six months now. It couldn't seem to make up its mind about giving up the ghost.

I decided I really wanted that drink. I had enjoyed me a few on the drive out. Then pitch in the Dentyne, which I could get wholesale any day of the week through my friendship with Big Fred at the Easy-Go. Fred was doing okay now. He'd survived the institutions. He was giving the nun battalion the same deals he gave me. Our families had been tight all the way back to our grandparents, which was as far back as anyone dared remember. There hadn't been any nuns around here in those days. There hadn't been much of anything, truth be told. Just endless, soggy fields and a horizon so low you could pitch up a hand and feel moisture dripping down the wrist.

I was back in the car by this while, having that drink.

Drinks.

The scarecrows, I noticed, had come down. Now I thought about it, it seemed to me a long time since I'd seen one. Used to be soybeans growing out here. Corn. Beans.

Grazing livestock. Then a new season and flat uninterrupted land stretching to distant wood lines. Now we had houses and town and highways and Subway and The Only Motel. Oh, my! My, my!

Our cherished Days of Yore. Such was the phrase occurring to me. My eyes wet, though don't get the idea sentimentality had anything to do with this onrush of tears. You could say any fondness I had for those olden days was in relapse. In disrepair. I still wanted to chomp down on someone's neck.

I had the dog's chawed shoe on the seat beside me. The tongue and heel was likely inside one of those dogs' bellies. In my line, you never know when you'll be needing evidence or how that evidence ought to constitute itself. I could look at that shoe and see CRIME written all over it. Which crime? What? Where? My evidence room was stacked with such as that.

The "V" vacancy sign was making spitting noises. The word, in big orange letters, was spaced all along The Only Motel's nine shed-like rooms. $19.95 the night. Hours negotiated. Wind had blown rags and fluff and plastic bags up there.

My Daddy and Big Fred had burnt down the other motel. That project had been the bright idea of some guy from Ohio. Bar, restaurant, disco, pool, fountains! Up in smoke, I tell you! Three days it took our volunteers to smother those flames.

About the same time in come three Greyhounds hauling those nuns. Into the lumber yard now known as the Olde Abby they move.

The dogs were back, scratching at my doors, licking my windows, showing me their teeth. George and Martha, if you want me to give those dogs a name.

I gave some thought to Viv in Buffalo buying that mattress. She liked firm, I liked soft.

I was exhausted, watching her sister throw those plates. I had to eat off those plates at home plus at Big Fred's, everywhere, don't ask me why. Dinnerware kept those girls afloat.

I had me a madman to nail, and somehow I knew that shoe on my seat featured in the crime. Anyway, my bottle was empty and I needed a bathroom.

I had a bit of the shakes but I was composed. Don't go thinking otherwise.

❧

Now it was back to the lock-up to chat with the madman.

But a detour was mandated. Today was payday for the caregivers. This little ditty popped into my head:

> *Sex was on a rampage*
> *whence it lay*
> *with love*
> *in dewy glen…*
> *Or could be plot*
> *took each the other's way.*
> *(So they say.)*

Such foolishness had lately been coming to me.

Leon Rooke

Sleeping Estella, dear Mum, had been bedridden through driven years. First the fire, then sickness slouching in. She'd been out of bed once in the past year, that time to see Christmas lights at the Olde Abby. The crèche. She had looked but hadn't seen. But she was pleased. Dee claimed she heard rumblings in her chest. We tried feeding her ice cream. Which was a mistake. Two churns were going the day hell broke loose.

Today was bath day. The caregivers had her in the shower stall, propped up on a stool. They had wrapped themselves in black garbage bags. Estelle seemed to be smiling. Perhaps she retained a memory of what water was.

I watched them carefully wash, rinse, and dry her hair. She had fine, lovely snow-white hair, the part that had grown back.

Later on, they would dress the bed, salve the roughened skin, powder her. They would ever be talking to her. They delighted in thinking sometimes she laughed. They were good at their job. They had the expertise.

"You drink that coffee," they kept telling me.

❧

The madman had ordered in dinner. He was sitting at a table with a red checkered-cloth top, in the company of a few of my boys. They were all chomping down on something I soon learned was duckling a la chipolata. Or *caneton a la chipolata*, as he called it. "Here's how Delores and I compose this dish," he was saying. "I quote to you from the sixth printing, 1961 edition of *Larousse Gastronomique.* 'Braise the duckling in the usual manner. When nearly done, drain and remove the trussing string. Return said duckling to the casserole, adding a chipolata garnish composed of ten braised chestnuts, ten glazed onions of rudimentary appearance, ten lean rashers of bacon, and eighteen lovely carrots diced to olive size. Boil down, please. Strain and pour. Over the duckling, of course. Cook. At the last moment, add exactly ten chipolata sausages.'"

He paused. He smiled. He was utterly mad.

He swung around. "Isn't that how you would do it, Racine?"

Racine was my hired help. She was on probation, coming three days a week to sweep and answer the phone. Her face was up between the bars, worshipful, it looked to me.

"More or less," she said. "It's the left-over lard gives me the headache."

"You're right," he said. "That precious lard! Duels have been fought over that lard."

The next minute the conversation had gone on to something else. The madman seemed intent on telling the gang how he and Deborah had initial inspiration for the *Bad Frog* book.

"We were strolling arm-in-arm through Jardins de l'avenue Foch, in Paris, when this bad frog hopped right between the legs of a passing nun. Wasn't that where it happened, Racine? In Foch? That startled nun?"

Leon Rooke

Racine had her body glued to the bars. "That's how I heard it," she said. "The whole thing is to my mind so – so like a thrilling movie."

I was in shock. My little sister had been to France? When? On her salary? How?

There you have it: a madman's world.

I had to take hold of myself. Thank God one of my boys had a pocket flask.

⚜

What I said to the madman was, "What are your intentions?"

He said, "With regard to what?"

"Those Wednesdays."

"Those Wednesdays are privileged," he said.

"Delores is practically underage," I said.

"She's older than a pile of monkeys," he said.

I thought about hitting him but was restrained by his bulk.

He went reflective. "It started with that *Frog* book," he said. "Delores had the idea my part of that book was biographical. Autobiographical, I mean. All that ridiculous business about my seduction of a nun. I asked her to name one instance when that book was such. She turned to page one. She read a few lines. 'Here you have this nun. Which nun, is what I want to know.' I was watching her eyes, how they skipped on ahead of what she was reciting. Then I watched her lips. I was hoping she'd recite the whole damn draft. So, in a manner of speaking, it was dating from those early precious seconds that *Frog* turned biographical. From that moment our lives were interwoven. Thus, the initiation of our Wednesdays. That's where our book was written, you know. Our Wednesdays at The Only Motel. Here," he said. "Have some duck."

"You're a madman," I said.

Some of the boys had to restrain me. I told him I meant siccing my dogs on him and if those dogs suffered mange and malaria and hydrophobia, if they foamed white at the mouth, then so much the better.

"You don't have dogs," he said. "Those dogs may run through your mind just the way you describe them, but those dogs were your crazy daddy's dogs and the whole kit and caboodle died ages ago, about the same time you were a barefoot boy limping around in barbed wire on a broken toe."

I tried choking him but we all know you can't shut up a madman. He was correct about the toe, the wire. He had neglected to mention the burnt hair, the boiling flesh.

"Yes," he said. "Yes. Your burns. Your father's lamp through the kitchen window just as the lot of you are pulling out your chairs to sit down to Sunday dinner. Grown-ups and children flying off every which way in their burning clothes. Thank God Delores and I were still in the sandbox. We will never know why your father decided to incinerate everyone. And it is perhaps true I was overzealous in my response to the current situation. An assault and battery charge might well be justified. I roughened him up a bit. I ripped up his Day Pass, took away the gas can, goose-stepped him back to the bus station. All right, maybe I singed his hair a little. Maybe – what is the phrase? – I employed 'excessive force.' After all, not for nothing am I known as a madman."

❧

What shall we eat, what may we drink, where shall we run when every river is on fire and toxic fumes haunt every breath?

Whose hands ply these oars? Who is that burning boy? Say you're into construction, reconstruction, resurrection, the pliable self redirected, improved, your body must be redesigned, restrung, other flesh grafted onto your own, ears rebuilt, nose, mouth, your very breath a sleek silent machine. The idea of a coming Sunday dinner is afloat – who is to sit down to that dinner, where will they sit, what will they eat, who is to cook, who shall wash the dishes, mop the floor? Sunday every day arrives, glory be to God, we are famished, hearth and hearty thanks to thee for this nourishment we now receive, sisters, please do sit down, will someone kindly call those lovely children in to dinner.

> *Nothing so firmly holds*
> *to truth*
> *as the boughs beyond*
> *my window*
> *swaying in wind.*

Look how those leaves
flutter each syllable
not one among billions
may comprehend.

CVC
Carter V. Cooper
SHORT FICTION ANTHOLOGY SERIES

Frank Westcott   Richard Van Camp
The Poet   *On the Wings of This Prayer*

Gregory Betts   Kristi-Ly Green
To Tell You   *The Patient*

Rishma Dunlop   Zoe Stikeman
Paris   *Single-celled Amoeba*

Silvia Moreno-Garcia   Leigh Nash
Scales as Pale as Moonlight   *The Field Trip*

Hugh Graham   Ken Stange
Through the Sky   *The Heart of a Rat*

SELECTED BY, AND WITH A PREFACE BY
Gloria Vanderbilt

CVC
Carter V. Cooper
SHORT FICTION ANTHOLOGY SERIES

Sean Virgo   Martha Bátiz
Grimava   *The Last Confession*

Darlene Madott   Christine Miscione
Writing (An Almost Love Story)   *Skin, Just*

Amy Stuart   Jacqueline Windh
The Boundless   *The Night the Floor Jumped*

Linda Rogers   Kris Bertin
Darling Boy   *Tom Stevie and Co.*

Daniel Perry   Phil Della
Mercy   *I Did It for You*

Kelly Watt
The Things My Dead Mother Says to Me

Leon Rooke
Here Comes Henrietta Armani

SELECTED BY, AND WITH A PREFACE BY
GLORIA VANDERBILT

Carter V. Cooper
Short Fiction Antholgy Series
~ BOOKS ONE THROUGH FOUR ~
46 stories that represent the best
of today's Canadian writing!

CVC
Carter V. Cooper
SHORT FICTION ANTHOLOGY SERIES

Austin Clarke   Priscila Uppal
They Never Told Me   *Cover Before Striking*

George McWhirter   Yakos Spiliotopoulos
Tennis   *Black Sheep*

Liz Windhorst Harmer   Greg Hollingshead
Teaching Strategies   *Mother Son*

Rob Peters   Matthew R. Loney
Sara's House   *A Fire in the Clearing*

Sang Kim   David Somers
When John Lennon Died   *Parsley Sells Out*

Helen Marshall
Lessons in the Raining of Household Objects

Leon Rooke
Constitutional Spheres of Everyday Life

SELECTED BY, AND WITH A PREFACE BY
GLORIA VANDERBILT

CVC
Carter V. Cooper
SHORT FICTION ANTHOLOGY SERIES — BOOK FOUR

Jason Timermanis   George McWhirter
Appetite   *Sixteen in Spokes*

Gregory Betts   Linda Rogers
Plank   *Three Strikes*

Hugh Graham   Matthew R. Loney
The Man   *The Pigeons of Peshawar*

Erin Soros   Kari Fisher
Morning is Vertical   *Saddle Up!*

Susan P. Redmayne   Madeline Sonik
Baptized   *Puncture*

Helen Marshall
The Zhanell Adler Brass Spyglass

Leon Rooke
Shits by a Madman

SELECTED BY, AND WITH A PREFACE BY
GLORIA VANDERBILT

Jason Timermanis of Toronto holds an MFA in Creative Writing from the University of Arizona. His work has appeared in *Spacing, Fab, Matrix*, and the anthology *Second Person Queer*. He is nearing the completion of his first novel. www.jasontimermanis.com

Hugh Graham of Toronto won an ACTRA and a Peabody Award for work with the CBC, has written for the *Walrus* and the *Toronto Star*, and his fiction has appeared in *Descant, ELQ/ Exile Quarterly, The Antigonish Review, The Fiddlehead* and *New Quarterly*. His shortlisted story "Through the Sky" appeared in the *Carter V. Cooper Short Fiction Anthology, Book One*. He has published two books, with Exile Editions: *Ploughing the Seas,* a first-person account of CIA operations in northern Costa Rica during the war in Nicaragua, and the gothic black comedy in dramatic form *Where the Sun Don't Shine*.

Helen Marshall of Sarnia, Ontario, is an author, editor, and bibliophile. Her debut collection, *Hair Side, Flesh Side*, won the 2013 British Fantasy Award. Her speculative poetry and fiction have appeared in anthologies and magazines, including *Paper Crow, The Year's Best Canadian Speculative Fiction and Poetry, The Year's Best Dark Fantasy and Horror* and the *Carter V. Cooper Short Fiction Anthology, Book Three*. Her short story collection *Gifts for the One Who Comes After* is forthcoming in 2014.

K'ari Fisher of Burns Lake, B.C., is currently following up on her degree in biology and studying writing at the University of Victoria. She is working on a collection of stories that explore the myopic vision of adolescence – the

close-up, cut-throat clarity that ironically struggles to pull things into big-picture focus. K'ari has short stories forthcoming in the *Malahat Review* and *Prairie Fire*.

Linda Rogers of Vancouver is a broadcaster, teacher, journalist, poet, novelist and songwriter. For her many books, she has received recognition by way of being awarded the Stephen Leacock prize for poetry, the Reuben Rose Poetry Prize (Israel), the Dorothy Livesay Award for best British Columbia book of poetry, the Hawthorne Poetry Prize, the Saltwater Festival prize, the People's Poetry Prize, and most recently was co-winner of *ELQ/Exile Quarterly*'s $2,500 Gwendolyn MacEwen Poetry Competition.

Susan P. Redmayne of Oakville, Ontario, is the author of offbeat fiction – her muse a talkative red-sided eclectus parrot named Merlin. She holds a degree in English Language and Literature from Western University and is an alum of the University of Toronto Faculty of  Law. In 2013 her short story "The Organ Grinder" was selected as a Top 3 finalist for the Penguin Random House Canada Student Award in Writing and appeared in *Three: Volume XI* edited by Lee Gowan. She is presently at work on a short story collection in which she explores diverse psychological responses to death and loss.

Matthew R. Loney of Toronto holds an MA in English and Creative Writing from the University of Toronto, and his stories have appeared in North American publications that include *Everything Is So Political*, *Writing Without Direction: 10 1/2 short stories by Canadian authors under 30* and the *Carter V. Cooper Short Fiction*

Anthology, Book Three. He recently published in India and Hong Kong. His first collection of stories, *That Savage Water*, will be published in autumn 2014.

Erin Soros of Vancouver has published fiction and non-fiction in international journals and anthologies, and her stories have been aired on the CBC and BBC as recipients of the CBC Literary Award, the Commonwealth Prize for the Short Story, and as a finalist for the BBC Short Story Award. "Still Water, B.C." was recently a finalist for the U.K.'s Costa Short Story Award. She also collaborates with other artists, studies philosophy, and teaches psycho-analysis, modern literature, and human rights.

Gregory Betts of St. Catharines, Ontario, is the author of five books of poetry, including *If Language, The Obvious Flap, Avant-Garde Canadian Literature: The Early Manifestations,* and the hilarious *This Is Importance: A Students' Guide to Canadian Literature.* His poems have  appeared in journals widely and internationally and his work is regularly taught at universities and high schools. He is the Director of the Centre for Canadian Studies and an Associate Professor in English at Brock University. His next book of poetry, *Boycott*, is forthcoming.

George McWhirter of Vancouver was born and raised in Belfast, Northern Ireland. He is the author of 10 books of poetry, eight books of short and long fiction, and four books of translation. Literary recognitions include the Commonwealth Poetry Prize (shared with Chinua Achebe), the Ethel Wilson Fiction Prize, and the F.R. Scott Translation Prize. He served as the inaugural Poet Laureate of Vancouver.

Madeline Sonik of Victoria, B.C. teaches writing at the University of Victoria. Her publications include a novel, a short story collection, a children's book, two poetry collections, and a volume of personal essays. She has co-edited three Canadian anthologies, and for her non-fiction has won the Annie Dillard Award for Creative Nonfiction, and was among 10 authors longlisted for the 2012 B.C. National Award for Canadian Non-fiction. She has also been a shortlist nominee for the 2012 Charles Taylor Prize and won the City of Victoria Butler Book Prize 2012.

**Leon Rooke** of Toronto is one of Canada's most prolific writers, and the author of over 20 books, among them *Shakespeare's Dog*, *The Fall of Gravity*, *A Good Baby*, *The Magician of Love*, *The Beautiful Wife*, *The Last Shot*, and *Wide World in Celebration and Sorrow: Acts of Kamikaze Fiction*. He has been widely anthologized, has won the Governor General's Award, and with John Metcalf annually runs the Metcalf-Rooke Award for short fiction.

The $15,000 Carter V. Cooper Short Fiction Competition

A perspective, from writer and artist Gloria Vanderbilt, who sponsors one of the largest literary prizes in Canada, and who supports this unique Canadians-only short fiction publication:

"I am proud and thrilled that all these wonderful writers are presented in the *CVC Anthology*. Carter, my son, Anderson Cooper's brother, was just 23 when he died in 1988. He was a promising editor, writer, and, from the time he was a small child, a voracious reader. When a child dies, just as his adult life is beginning, in addition to the overwhelming grief, his family and friends are left with many unanswerable questions. I often wonder what would he be doing? What kind of man would he have become? If Carter were alive he would be 49 years old now. Some things are not knowable, of course, but I do know Carter would still be in love with writing, with words, and with stories. Carter came from a family of storytellers, and stories were a guide which helped him discover the world. Though I, and those who loved Carter, still hear his voice in our heads and in our hearts, my son's voice was silenced long ago. I hope this prize helps other writers find their voice, and helps them touch others' lives with the mystery and magic of the written word."

The Year Five competition opens Monday, October 13, 2014, and closes for submissions on Monday, March 30, 2015.

There is also a special publishing follow through from this literary endeavour, and that is the publication of full-length books by authors who have made the shortlist. See following pages.

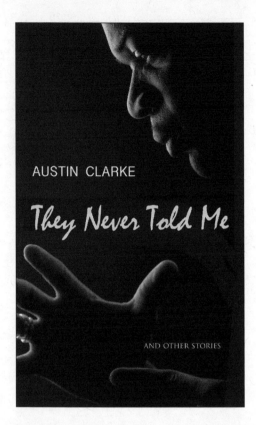

AUSTIN CLARKE

They Never Told Me

AND OTHER STORIES

CVC YEAR THREE WINNER

From the winner of the Giller, Commonwealth, Trillium and Writers' Trust prizes, comes an outstanding collection of eight stories.

"[The book has] a fidelity to the kind of sensual language that has always been a hallmark of the author's writing." —*National Post*

"While many of these stories are stationed in memory of the new immigrant experience, the titular story strikes a harmony of hurt as an elderly Barbadian immigrant stumbles around Toronto in black-face, lost in a fog of nostalgia, his struggle with age resurrecting and reciprocating his struggle with racism. The parallel is just the tip of the iceberg of insight Clarke's wisdom offers in these stories."
— *Telegraph Journal*

2013 autumn release   5 x 8   212 pages $19.95

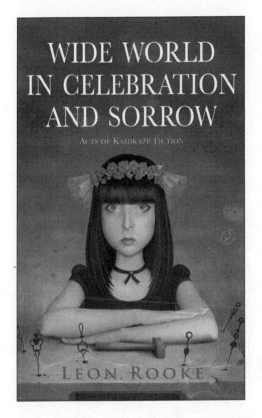

"The 20 pieces that make up *Wide World in Celebration and Sorrow: Acts of Kamikaze Fiction* could be considered a kind of literary tasting menu for those unfamiliar with Rooke's oeuvre... and many of Rooke's signature registers – the absurdist humour, the literary and philosophical allusiveness, the sudden violence – are on display [and...] interact with each other as readily as with a reader."
—*National Post*

2012 autumn release   5.5 x 8.5   272 pages $19.95

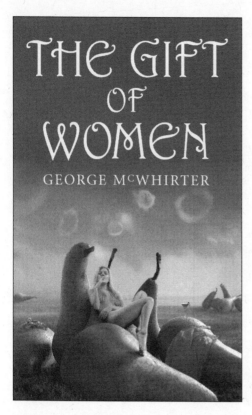

George McWhirter grounds his delightful characters in the real, while his sharp wit and creative scenarios border on the fantastical. A woman adopts a dolphin-man, an Irish madam runs a railroad bordello in the desert, a drought-stricken river joins a jobless man on his way to the pub for a pint of solace, a Catholic woman's seventh child, son of a seventh daughter, is left to the mercy of five convent-schooled sisters. *The Gift of Women* is about sexuality and religion, the surreal and the magical, tales of earthy and incendiary women, capable of setting a man, the Alberni Valley and all of Vancouver Island on fire.

2014 autumn release   5 x 8   256 pages, french flaps $19.95

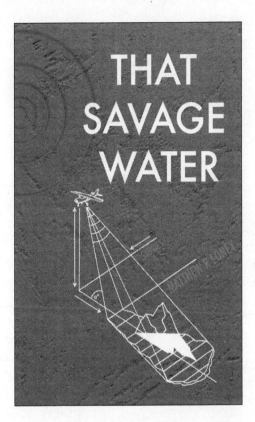

THAT SAVAGE WATER

That Savage Water is a striking collection of stories about travels abroad, told in language that is rich in description, full of lucid and lively textures, smells and sensations that transports the reader to places not on the average itinerary. From familiar departure lounges on to foreign cities steeped in history, the enticing turquoise beaches of picture-perfect postcards, the desolate mountain ranges that take one well off the beaten track, bathing in the sacred Ganges, and fringe indulgences in Cambodian brothels – and a return to a northern Canadian cabin where the father of a tsunami victim contemplates how a surge of savage water forever changed the lives of so many, most poignantly, his own.

2014 autumn release   5 x 8   208 pages, french flaps $19.95

"Moreno-Garcia has a spare prose style, but it is one that belies the complexity and depth of her ideas and is well suited to the many common folk who populate her stories. There is a subtlety and seriousness amid the skulls and bones, and beauty among the omens and death." —*The Winnipeg Review*

Spanning a variety of genres – fantasy, science fiction, horror – and time periods, Silvia Moreno-Garcia's exceptional debut collection features short stories infused with Mexican folklore, yet firmly rooted in a reality that transforms as the fantastic erodes the rational.

2012 autumn release   Fiction   5 x 8   224 pages $18.95

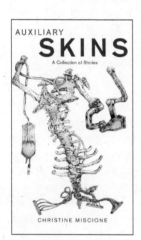

"Miscione excels at writing about horrible things in beautiful ways. Her prose is not only deft and neat, but often wrenchingly lovely, so that much of the text comes across like a suppurating wound wrapped in hand-stitched lace." —*Quill & Quire*

A remarkable first collection. Existing somewhere in that chasm between bodily function and souled-ness, Christine Miscione's debut collection *Auxiliary Skins* illumines all that's perilous, beautiful and raw about being human.

2012 autumn release   Fiction   5 x 8   160 pages $16.95